THE
SHIELD

THE
SHIELD

A. WALTER PUBLISHING COMPANY

Cover Design: Karri Klawiter
Interior Illustrations: M.T. Zimny
Editing: E&A Editing Services
Book Design and Typesetting: Enchanted Ink Publishing

The text type was set in Garamond Premier Pro

ISBN: 979-8-9912454-0-1 (E-book)
ISBN: 979-8-9912454-1-8 (Paperback)

Thank you for your support of the author's rights.

WWW.ALEXASHAYS.COM

I dedicate this book to my grandma, Charlotte.

Ever since I was a little girl, I said I would
dedicate my first book to my grandma,
who always believed in and supported me.

This is for you, Grandma. I love you.

ALEXA SHAY

THE
SHIELD

BOOK ONE OF THE SHIELD SERIES

PROLOGUE

The Spirit

"We did it, Shield. We—" Anna coughed violently.

"*Conserve your energy.*" Blood trickled from the side of her host's mouth, which was currently her mouth too. The warm liquid slid down their neck and numbness spread through their limbs. She commanded their body to move but nothing happened. The gray sky above them grew unfocused and blinking didn't help.

"I knew what I was gettin' into, and I know I'm dyin.'" Anna coughed again, quieter this time.

"*You did well. All living beings are safe thanks to you, Anna.*"

"Yer right about that." Their mouth pulled up at the sides for a moment before going slack. A great wrenching sensation engulfed the spirit before she was jerked from her host and thrust into darkness.

*Y*OU GET TOO ATTACHED TO YOUR HOSTS." THE RASPY voice snapped her back to consciousness. She opened her ethereal senses, homing in on her enemy. The transition from host to ether was jarring. Cold tendrils brushed her awareness, and she mentally shoved them back.

"What do you want?" she responded.

"You are illogical, all light beings are. Mortals die, I do not understand why you get attached. One is much like the other."

If she could sigh in this form, she would have. She settled for attempting a sigh-like sound in their link and failed. She missed having lungs. *"You would never understand. Your purpose is to kill life and light, but I will stop you every time."*

Its grating laughter jarred her. *"I only need to win once, and I can do this forever. Humans multiply infinitely, and our hosts' lines have always been bountiful. I will burn through bodies until I destroy you."* It vanished, cackling. She missed having eyes to roll.

She sent a shaking sensation through her form, attempting to recreate the feeling of casting off water when she was in her host's body. Darkness soon slipped across her awareness, and she drifted into hibernation.

*S*HE AWOKE WITH A BOLT OF TERROR. SHARDS OF glass flew by her face, and she reflexively cast a golden shield of energy around herself as the strange box she was in imploded. The screech of rending metal became her world, and screams pierced her ears. Hands covered them, hands she had not commanded. *What is this?*

Within the safety of her golden sphere, she looked down at small, outstretched arms. The hands and arms were pale and freckled.

BANG.

The box around them shuddered and everything ceased. The silence was deafening.

The consciousness she'd accidentally shunted aside stirred.

"This is too soon."

"M-mommy? Daddy?" her body whimpered.

"All will be well, child." Reaching inward, the spirit put the little girl to sleep. Her body drifted gently into the wreckage, slumping forward when it landed.

I'M GONNA BE LATE!" AMY YELLED WHILE GRAB-bing her keychain-covered backpack from her bedroom floor. Her long, wet brown hair slapped her cheeks as she jogged into the hallway, leaving behind cold streaks of water. "Bye, Arty, love you!" Throwing open the front door, she ran out.

She raced down the apartment building's stairs and sprinted to her bus stop, breath burning in her chest. Her legs ached from the exertion, and her black, rainbow-doodled Converse splashed in the few shallow puddles she couldn't dodge.

Great, I just got the design right. This'd better not be a bad omen for today. Ugh, now my jeans are wet too.

She skittered to a stop as the bus pulled up.

The driver smiled at her as she opened the door, and Amy waved in reply before scooting into the first empty seat and pressing her face against the cool glass of the window.

Once her lungs stopped aching, she pulled her phone out of the pocket of her jeans to scroll aimlessly on her socials, catching up on what she'd missed. Her feed was more artists than classmates, and she couldn't help but roll her eyes at a recent update from one of them. *Of course Janie's relationship status is "it's complicated," they fight non-stop. They should just break up.* Once she grew bored of scrolling, she checked the weather for the weekend and smiled at the little sun on the screen. Sun was exactly what she wanted for her sweet sixteen.

When the bus pulled up to school, she made her way inside. Bodies bumped into her, as she kept her eyes downcast as much as possible, curling into herself. Crowds were the worst sometimes. She caught a flash of neon when forced to look up and walked over to a colorfully clad girl.

"Hey Satomi," she said.

The girl turned and grinned, the jarring fluorescent lights washing out her golden undertones. Satomi was a blur of pink as she wrapped herself around Amy like she hadn't just seen her yesterday. Her chin-length black hair had electric pink and blue tips that seemed brighter in the poor lighting, about the only benefit of the nasty tube lights. Amy stooped a little to return her hug with gusto.

"Good morning, Ames." Satomi gushed as she stepped back. "My parents *finally* said I could come to your birthday this weekend." She hung on to Amy's arm, and they walked down the hall toward Mrs. Sanchez's.

"That's awesome." Amy looked at her with a wide smile, then slammed into a body that felt much bigger than hers.

She fell back, a searing pain shooting up her arm where her body had made contact. A golden light flashed across her vision, and her cheeks began their telltale burn, which meant she was turning crimson.

"I am *so* sorry!" she exclaimed, manners overriding confusion. She looked up into cold, emerald-green eyes. She'd run into a very tall and, apparently, very grumpy boy who was glaring at her wordlessly. She wasn't sure if she'd noticed him around school before. He kept his eyes locked on hers for several long seconds before turning and walking away.

"You okay?" Satomi asked, reaching out a hand.

Amy sat frozen. Something stirred inside her, and she wondered if she was going to throw up. Staring at the boy's retreating back, she couldn't miss the elegant way he carried himself and how the crowd seemed to unconsciously melt out of his path. Had she really never seen him before?

"Sorry. I wasn't paying attention." Amy stood with little help from Satomi and brushed off her jeans before rubbing the arm he'd hit. It no longer hurt.

"What a jerk. He didn't even ask if you were okay."

"It's whatever. I have more important things to worry about." She gulped. "Like the upcoming presentation." Speaking the words out loud caused butterflies to take flight in her abdomen, and she felt sick again. Satomi patted her arm, her eyes understanding. She grabbed Amy again and half dragged her to class.

"Good morning Mrs. Sanchez," Amy and Satomi said together as they entered.

"Good morning, girls. Please take your seats."

Amy took her seat between Adam and Satomi's desks. Adam flipped his blond hair out of his eyes as she sat down. His stocky frame looked even bigger behind the school desk.

"You been thinking about the Tolo dance?" he asked in lieu of a greeting. "Since you girls have to do the asking for once."

"Dances aren't really my thing." Amy turned to Satomi. "What about you? You asking anyone to Tolo?"

"I'm not sure I'm going either," she replied. "I've heard there's a poetry reading happening downtown that night."

"Dances are way too normal for you," Adam teased. Amy smacked him on the arm. "What?"

"You're being rude," she said. Satomi remained silent but gave Adam a withering look. "Has any girl dared to ask the 'Whittaker Prince' to the dance?" Adam flushed.

The bell on Mrs. Sanchez's desk dinged. "Hello, class," she said. "It's time for your presentations on *To Kill a Mockingbird*. We'll be going in alphabetical order."

Amy's stomach churned and her hands shook. Being toward the end of the alphabet sucked almost as badly as being at the beginning because of the waiting. Her lungs felt tight, and she rubbed her hands up and down her thighs, trying to calm herself, but the smooth texture of the denim did little to help ground her.

Sammi Roche stood to present, which meant Amy *Sanders* was next. She felt her face already getting hot and began to squirm. Tears tried to form, and she furiously rubbed her eyes. Reading her notes again did nothing to help. The words blended together, and she couldn't remember anything she had written or practiced last night.

"Amy," Mrs. Sanchez called. "It's your turn."

Amy stood and her knees shook.

Those three minutes in front of the class definitely lasted an hour. She stumbled over her words, forgot things, and got details mixed up. A few giggles could be heard, and she wished for the ground to open and swallow her whole. She wasn't sure what happened after the giggles, it was like her mind went blank and her body went on autopilot. When it was finally over, she resisted the urge to run to her seat and walked jerkily back. Once there, she put her head in her hands and stared at the desk in front of her until the bell rang.

Amy grabbed her bag and bolted out the door followed closely by Satomi.

"I failed," Amy moaned. A pit formed in her stomach and her eyes burned with tears again. "My grade's gonna tank."

"It'll be okay," Satomi said, putting an arm around her shoulder. "It wasn't worth as many points as a test."

"You don't understand." Amy shoved her hands through her hair, knocking Satomi's arm away. "I have to get good grades to get into Clearwater. I *have to*. They're the best art institute in the country, and they only take a few hundred new students each year, and I *need* to get in. It's the only thing I've ever wanted."

Satomi spun Amy around, stopping her. "I know how badly you want to go to Clearwater. I do too. But bombing one thing isn't going to stop an artist like you from getting into an art school like that." Satomi's tone was firm. "Your portfolio will knock their socks off, so take a breath."

THE FRONT DOOR OPENED AS AMY PLACED A CASserole on a hot pad in the middle of the small, round dining table. It bore several scuff marks in the warm brown finish from the many family dinners they'd had when their parents were alive and all the ones that came after.

"Welcome home, Arty," she said with forced cheerfulness as he closed the door and set his bag down. His hair was messy, a clear sign he'd had a long day. *Great.*

"So. Vanessa called…"

"Oh?" Amy asked, aiming for nonchalance. *I don't care how long he's known her, hearing him call Mrs. Sanchez by her first name will always be weird.*

"She said something about a presentation… anything you want to talk about?"

Amy sighed. "I bombed my presentation today. I just froze, it was a nightmare. My GPA is gonna drop."

Arty laughed. "Your grades are great, you're stressing too much. Not everyone can be good at public speaking. She passed you, but you might want to try to snag some extra credit where you can. She said she knew you tried your best, and your grade will reflect that." Amy blew out another sigh. "She knew you'd be upset. That's why she called me."

Amy felt lighter as they sat down at the table and began to dish up dinner.

2
The Boy

THE BOY FUSSED WITH HIS HAIR IN THE MIRror to get it to lie right, emerald-green eyes staring back at him as he picked off any stray lint from his clothes. Finally, he smoothed his shirt once and turned away. He struggled to hide the tremble in his hands as he strode across the large house, each step as loud as a gunshot.

He knocked three times on a dark, polished door, waiting until he heard a voice calling for him to come in. He schooled his face into impassiveness before turning the doorknob and entering a richly furnished office. He went to stand in front of a desk, facing the back of a large leather chair.

"Were you successful?"

All the saliva dried up in his mouth as the churning in

his stomach intensified. "Yes, Father. She is the one we are looking for."

"Excellent." The man didn't look up. "Keep an eye on her, but don't make further contact until we tell you to. Everything rests on your shoulders."

"Yes, sir."

"You may leave."

The boy turned on his heel and opened the door again, then carefully closed it behind him. A bead of sweat trickled down his face, which he wiped away. After only a few seconds of deep breathing, he straightened, his face once again becoming blank as he walked back down the hall.

3

Amy

"HAPPY BIRTHDAY!" ARTY YELLED FROM BE-hind Amy.

Jumping with a squeal, she turned around to look at him, mouth agape. Her heart beat hard as an odd sensation shuddered through her body. A golden light flashed through the kitchen, and the sensation vanished.

"What was that?" Arty gasped as he looked around.

"Power surge?" Amy rubbed her arms. Nothing felt weird now.

"Whatever, nothing seems to have blown up. As I was saying, happiest of birthdays to my wonderful, perfect baby sister." He scooped her up in a big hug and twirled her around.

"Knock it off." Amy shoved him, and he set her down. She straightened her shirt and flipped back her hair. "You're so weird. What's the big thing on the table?" It was obviously a rainbow wrapped present, but what could be that big?

"A birthday present, open it! You have to open it before we can do anything else." Bubbles of excitement rushed through her and she smiled as she sat down, bouncing slightly in the seat.

She tore the paper to pieces, relishing the sound.

On the table before her was a tan wicker basket with brown buckles. "An *actual* picnic basket?" She squealed as she opened it and saw a full set of dishware for four inside along with a red and white checkered blanket. It reminded her of the ones from the cartoon *Yogi Bear* that she loved when she was little. "We can use it today!"

"I'm glad you like it. Everything's washed and ready to go. Do we have anything else to do besides pack the food? I want to do everything so that you can enjoy your special day."

"Nah, just the food. You make the potato salad, and I'll get the Tofurky sandwiches? I've already packed chopped fruits, veggies, and snacks."

"Yup, I'm on it."

***

A SIGN WITH THE WORDS "WHITTAKER HILLS PARK" in white, hand-painted letters was held up over the entrance by two weathered poles, worn but beautiful. Similar signs were at each park entrance, but this one was Amy's favorite. Memories of past visits briefly flashed through her mind as they did every time she saw it.

Amy's leg bounced as the car came to a stop, and she

fumbled trying to get her seatbelt off. The lights in the car flickered.

"I hope nothing's wrong with Picard," Arty muttered as he patted the car's dash. Amy rolled her eyes while undoing her buckle.

"I'm sure he's fine," she said. "Hurry up, we need to go!" She threw open the door and then popped the trunk to grab the picnic basket, but Arty playfully wrenched it from her hands. "Hey, I was gonna carry that!"

"You're the birthday girl, I'm carrying *everything*," he said, brushing her out of the way. She lost her footing, windmilled her arms, and thumped gracelessly onto her butt. A brilliant light flashed as the pain flared. Arty gasped and stumbled back, barely keeping the basket in his arms.

"You okay?" Amy asked, looking up at his frazzled face. That strange swirling feeling erupted in her stomach again, as if something was alive inside of her.

"For a second, it felt like something was burning me. Maybe the sun reflected off something?" The feeling passed. Arty looked down at her, gasped, and helped her up while apologizing profusely.

They unloaded the car after a little more fussing from Arty, and then made their way to the picnic area. Amy broke into a run when she saw her two best friends waiting at a decorated picnic table. "Satomi! Adam!"

There were tons of blue and silver balloons and streamers tied everywhere. Satomi and Adam were frowning at each other, but both smiled when they saw her charging toward them. Amy tackled Satomi with a big hug, and they fell into the grass as they embraced. Adam walked to Arty, taking some of the load from his arms.

"It looks great," Amy said as she surveyed the decorations. "I love it." The blues complimented each other and were set off nicely by the silver. *Must have been more Satomi's work than Adam's.*

Adam came over and gave her a hug that felt like he was trying to crush her, and she pulled away quickly. "I'm stoked to eat, I'm starving," he said.

Amy glanced at the table to check out her birthday cake. It read "Happy 16th Birthday Amy THEBESTSISTER-EVER!" in deep purple frosting. She shook her head at it, then snapped a picture of the table before aiming the phone at everyone, all of them posing instantly. "Gotta take pics before we mess everything up," she said as she reached for a sandwich.

Satomi made a mess eating, as usual, and Adam grimaced. "Do you have to do that?" he finally blurted out.

"Do what?" Satomi asked, tilting her head to the side as crumbs fell from her face.

"Eat like that, it's gross."

Satomi opened her mouth, but Amy said, "Just don't look, Adam. Leave her be."

"Fine, fine."

Satomi went back to eating, her cheeks pink.

When everyone was done, Arty took the plastic cover off the cake and placed sixteen brightly colored candles into it. The group sang an off-key rendition of "Happy Birthday." Heat traveled all the way to Amy's hairline as she waited for the song to end. She closed her eyes. *I wish to not be embarrassed so easily.* Then she took a deep breath and blew out the candles.

Contentment settled into her chest as she looked around at her favorite people. She resisted the urge to grin while chewing a mouthful of cake. It was yellow with fudge frosting like all of her birthday cakes before it.

Finally, it was time for presents. Satomi thrust her neon-blue wrapped present into Amy's hands. "Mine first!" she yelled.

Amy tore the paper and uncovered a photo album with pictures of them together as far back as kindergarten by the looks of it. She teared up instantly. *So many memories.* She flipped through the first few pages. "I can't wait to look at every single picture," she said to Satomi, who beamed back at her.

Adam's present of a gift card gave her a much-needed break from strong emotions.

A blush spread across Amy's cheeks yet again as Arty surrounded her with several gifts, making her feel like she was under a spotlight. He got her a big stack of different sized canvases and high-quality paintbrushes. She hadn't told him she'd needed anything, but he had noticed. The warmth of feeling loved washed over her.

The last present from Arty she opened was a white jewelry box. She looked at him with a raised eyebrow, and he smiled but said nothing. Inside the box was a silver, heart-shaped locket with a tiny diamond chip in the middle. It was perfectly to her taste. She slid her thumbnail into the side and popped it open.

Inside were two pictures that made Amy's eyes refill with tears. On the left side was a picture of her parents on their wedding day, young and smiling. A single tear rolled down her cheek as she looked at them. She could see Arty's chin in their dad's face and their matching blue eyes in her mom's. *What would they have said today? Where would we have celebrated?* Her heart ached.

The other picture was Amy and Arty from her first day of kindergarten. It was her favorite picture of the two of them together. She grinned, recalling the chaos. Arty had a very awkward look on his face that she now recognized as bewilderment, and she had on a mismatched outfit with a huge smile, her pigtails uneven and messy. Arty had been doing his best. She wiped her tears, squashing down the wistful thoughts of her parents, and she threw her arms around him.

"Thank you, Arty," she said as he hugged her back. "It's perfect. Can you put it on me?"

He took the locket from her, and she moved her hair so he could fasten it. It hung just below her collar bone. She touched it as she smiled up at him, seeing unshed tears in his eyes.

T HIS WAS GREAT," SATOMI SAID, PICKING BLADES OF grass and braiding them. The sun cast long shadows on the ground where they sat. Amy nodded as she picked her own strands of grass to braid. Arty excused himself to walk across the open area to the bathrooms.

"I think I'm gonna head out." Adam's expression was similar to the bored look he wore in math.

"So soon?" Amy stood and brushed herself off, turning toward him.

"Yeah, some of the guys on the team are having a party I wanna go to."

"Of course you'd rather party with the 'cool' kids than stay here. What a *great* friend." Satomi glared at Adam, her cheeks splashed with red.

"Well yeah, I'm a Whittaker after all. Gotta give the people what they want."

Amy looked at him in disbelief. *What a pompous thing to say. I hate it when his family's expectations make him act out like this.*

"Poor Adam Whittaker," Satomi said with obvious disdain. "It must be *so* hard to have so many obligations."

"Hey, man, it is hard. You don't know what I have to live up to. You don't know anything about me." His voice was getting loud as his face turned a mottled red.

She shot to her feet. "I know that you're pretentious and—"

"Satomi! Adam!" Amy shouted to get their attention. "Can you not ruin my birthday, please? I only get one a year." Her attempt at humor fell flat.

"I don't have to take this." Adam stormed off toward the parking area.

"Adam!" Amy yelled, but he didn't turn around. She looked at Satomi, whose now splotchy face was screwed up like she was about to cry. "Satomi?" she asked. "What the heck was that? That was rude."

"He started it! You know what, I'm going home too," Satomi choked out as she turned and ran toward the bus stop. "I'm sorry we ruined your birthday." Amy could hear a sob come from her as she ran away. Amy stood there, frozen.

"What happened? Where is everyone?" Arty walked up, his eyes looking a little bloodshot and puffy. Amy gaped at him, all the warm feelings from earlier flooding out of her to be replaced with confusion and a slowly building anger.

AMY SLAMMED HER BEDROOM DOOR BEHIND HER, throwing herself onto the bed and burying her face in her pillow. Her phone dinged, but she ignored it. *Those jerks can buzz off, I'm not dealing with their crap.* They'd ruined her sweet sixteen, and they could deal with her silence. *They knew how excited I was. Why couldn't they keep it together for one afternoon?*

It dinged about a dozen more times. Groaning, she finally reached into her pocket and jerked it out to see a barrage of texts.

Satomi: Amy, I'm sorry.

Satomi: Can we talk?

Satomi: 😭

Satomi: 😭 😭 😭

Amy: Leave me alone.

Adam texted her similarly, without all the emojis, and he received the same response. Amy turned off her phone and tossed it into her hamper.

She went to grab a book from her bookshelf, which meant shoving several knick-knacks and miniature sculptures out of her way.

She spent the rest of her "sweet" sixteen grumpily finishing her reading for English, then got ahead on the rest of her homework. *My birthday may be ruined by those jerks, I might as well not let my grades suffer for it.* She had a hard time concentrating as her mind kept drifting back to the stupid fight from earlier. *What even started all this?*

Arty knocked on her door.

"Come in," she said.

He opened the door and took a seat on her bed.

"Do you want to talk?" he asked.

"I don't know what there is to talk about. My two *best* friends hate each other more than they love me. They couldn't even keep it together for a few hours so I could enjoy my birthday. It's stupid, and they pissed me off!" She finished the last bit of her outburst in almost a yell. She took a deep breath—yelling would upset their neighbors.

"Any idea why they hate each other?"

"No! That's what makes it so frustrating. Satomi never acts like that toward anyone. She's said that Adam only pretends to be nice around me, but why? I imagine Adam hates her because she accuses him of being two-faced. Sometimes I wonder if she's jealous I have another friend now. I have no idea what their problem is, and I'm getting sick of it." She threw her hands up, and the lights flickered.

"Why do I get the feeling we're not in Kansas anymore," Arty mumbled.

Amy glared at him. "You watch too many weird shows."

"You *like* some of those weird shows. Besides, weird stuff has been happening all week."

Amy jumped up and struck a heroic pose. "I'm developing superpowers and transforming into Supergirl." She climbed onto her bed. "Watch me fly!" She leapt, one fist extended, looking like a lame superheroine as she stumbled at the landing. She rounded on Arty. "Do you hear how stupid you sound?" she said. "I have real problems with my two dumb friends."

Arty chuckled. "I suppose it was a bit of a wild thought."

"Darn right it was."

"Have you talked to either of them since we got home?" Amy told him about the texts. "I think it was smart to give yourself some time to cool down. How's about we do something fun tomorrow, just the two of us?"

"I'd like that." It'd be nice if her birthday weekend wasn't total garbage.

"Perfect! I'm going to bed. Go to bed soon, okay? Weekends don't mean you can stay up all night, even if it's your birthday."

Amy rolled her eyes. "Okay, whatever, night."

Arty shut the door behind him, and Amy flopped onto her bed.

"They're both *so* stupid," she moaned into the pillow as irritation bubbled through her.

THE LIGHTS IN THE APARTMENT FLICKERED AS SHE bustled about getting ready for bed. "Darn, faulty wiring," she mumbled around her toothbrush. She glared at the light bulb in the bathroom. Focusing all her ire on it, something heated within her. The light flickered again, then exploded with a brilliant flash, sending glass everywhere.

Amy closed her eyes and screamed as she held up her hands to shield herself. Her toothbrush fell, and she heard glass tinkle around her. Her heart pounded in her ears. Another blinding flash of light filled the air, and a burning smell filled her nose.

"Amy!" Arty wrenched the door open. Amy looked up at him, his form backlit by the hallway light. "What happened?" He looked from the shattered glass at her feet to the broken light fixture on the wall.

"I-I don't know!" she exclaimed as toothpaste foam flew from her mouth. "I-I was looking at that light, and it just burst!" Arty stared at her.

"So... you were staring at a light? And it... exploded? On its own?"

"Yeah!" She nodded vigorously. More foam dribbled from her mouth, but she was too shocked to do anything about it.

"It must have been some sort of short. Hold still while I go get the broom." Arty turned off the light switch and left.

Amy looked down at the damage. A perfect circle of glass surrounded her feet, illuminated by the hallway light. She kicked the glass before Arty could get back, not wanting him to notice how weird it was. *What the heck happened?*

When he got back, he handed her a pair of pink bunny slippers before sweeping up the glass.

Amy lay in bed for a long time that night. Goose bumps pricked along her arms as she focused on the sensation of something moving within her, trying to pinpoint where it was coming from. *What's happening to me?*

4

Amy

AMY'S RETRO ALARM CLOCK WENT OFF, JARRING her out of the recurring nightmare of her parents' deaths. She could have sworn there was a voice in it this time, but everything was foggy. Exhausted, she stood up and smacked the clock, jumping as the sound of cracking plastic filled her ears. She stared at it in shock, heart pounding. The time still glowed red, but the blue case around it was covered in cracks.

"It was super old," she said to herself, not sounding very sure. Several deep breaths helped the buzzing in her head stop.

She tried to distract herself, but thinking of seeing her friends made her stomach ache after she had studiously ignored them all weekend. She put on her new locket and grabbed her backpack before heading to the kitchen.

"Hungry?" Arty asked, pouring cereal into a bowl.

"I should probably eat something, huh?" she asked with forced cheer and a fake smile. Arty frowned.

He shoved toast at her. "I know you're anxious about seeing them, but it'll all work out." The toast felt and tasted like gritty cardboard, but Amy forced it down.

"I'm going to catch the bus," she said with more forced cheer. "Have a good day."

Amy trotted down the stairs and to the bus stop. *What am I going to say to them?* She had first period homeroom with Satomi and Adam, so she would have to start the day by facing them. Maybe that was better than dreading it all day long. Her stomachache was back.

The school bus pulled up and she took the first empty seat, like always. Her stomach fluttered with nerves. Something inside her moved. Freezing, she inspected the strange sensation. It was like something uncoiling within her. She wrapped her arms around her middle and pressed her face to the cold glass of the window. As she breathed, the stirring ceased. She closed her eyes and focused on her breathing. In and out.

The school bus pulled up to the high school much too quickly, so she loitered outside of the school, waiting until the last minute to rush into Mrs. Sanchez's room with about thirty seconds to spare. The old woman glanced up from her desk and smiled when she saw Amy, her tanned skin crinkling.

"Good morning, dear. Did you have a good birthday?"

"It was good...in the beginning," she said stiffly. "Arty got me this locket," she added, more loosely as she took off the pendant and handed it to her teacher. Mrs. Sanchez covered her mouth with a trembling hand.

"This is beautiful," she said. Her voice and hands continued to tremble as her eyes filled with tears that she quickly dashed away as she handed the locket back to Amy. "I'm so glad he thought to give it to you."

"I love it." Amy flashed her first real smile since her disastrous birthday party. The bell rang, and she took her seat between Satomi and Adam, not looking at either of them. Suddenly, she wished that she had worn her hair down so she could cover her face and not see them at all. Sadly, it hadn't been cooperating enough for that.

Amy barely heard anything Mrs. Sanchez said all period. The hour seemed to take forever with Satomi and Adam randomly trying to get her attention, but she refused to acknowledge them, staring straight ahead at the board. When the bell rang, she almost tipped over her desk in her hurry to exit the classroom.

"Ames, wait!" Satomi called from behind her. Amy glanced back and saw Satomi running after her, one hand outstretched. She tried desperately to get through the crowd of slow-moving teenagers. *Why does everyone feel the need to walk in a straight line across the hall like some kind of traveling blockade?*

"Amy!" Satomi yelled again, this time catching Amy's arm and spinning her around. "Amy, talk to me. Please." Amy looked at Satomi, her arms trembling with her desire to escape. Satomi panted and tears formed in her eyes. "I'm so, so sorry. I didn't mean to ruin your birthday, I really didn't! Please don't hate me!" The tears overflowed. She let go and wiped her eyes.

Amy sighed, her shoulders slumping forward. "I don't

hate you, I just haven't been ready to talk to you. I still love you, but what the heck was that?"

Satomi fidgeted before taking a deep breath. "Okay, so don't get mad—"

"It's a little late for that."

"Fair," Satomi replied. "The thing is, Adam isn't always a very nice person when you're not around. It's annoying to imagine you ending up with someone like that. He's—" Amy doubled over in a coughing fit as she inhaled too fast. Satomi jumped.

"What do you mean 'ending up with'?!" she almost shouted. She quieted herself as people stared at them. "What are you talking about?" she finished in a strangled whisper. "Adam is *just* a friend!"

Satomi gawked at her. "You haven't noticed?"

"Noticed what?"

"The way he looks at you," Satomi answered with obvious disgust. "He looks at you like you're something shiny he can buy."

"I've never noticed anything, and I don't like him that way at all."

Satomi sighed. "I'm sorry, I shouldn't have said that. Maybe I'm imagining it. Are we... are we okay? I'll try to do better at not letting him get to me."

"And I'll try better to keep an eye on him." The two paused and then hugged each other tightly, moving together simultaneously.

"I missed you *so* much, that was the longest weekend of my *life*," Satomi almost sobbed.

"I missed you too."

Amy looked up from her lunch to see Adam sauntering toward her and Satomi. He was forced to pause every few feet by someone trying to talk to him, but he smiled and waved each person off. Satomi focused resolutely on her lunch as he got closer, but Amy stared into his eyes as he stopped at their table. Her stomach started to burn as she fought the urge to look away.

Adam was the first to break eye contact. He cleared his throat while running a hand through his hair. "Um, I'm sorry for being a jerk at your birthday."

"And?" Amy said coldly. Her fists were clenched and shaking under the table and her legs wanted to flee, but she valiantly fought the urge to back down. *It's the right thing to do. Stay strong.*

He sighed. "And I'm sorry to you too, Satomi. I was out of line."

Satomi looked up. "I'm sorry for being rude too," she said, and then went back to her food. Amy exhaled, her stomach still queasy. *That's probably as good as it's going to get.*

"It's okay," Amy said, the earlier icy feeling melting slightly. "Would you like to sit with us?" She unclenched her hands and gestured at the empty chairs around the table.

"Sorry, I already sat down with the guys. Do you wanna hang out later this week? Maybe a movie?" He flashed a winning smile.

"Sure, we can probably hang out. Let me know."

"Okay, see you around."

He walked back to his table as Amy waved goodbye. She looked over at Satomi. "I'm proud of you."

Satomi laughed. "Thanks, I think? We should hurry up. I wanna get to art class early to start my sculpture." Amy felt lighter than she had in days. *Things are looking up.*

5

Amy

FTER EXITING THE BUS, AMY RAN TO HER apartment and threw open the door. She skidded to a halt, a scream freezing in her throat as adrenaline flooded her veins. A woman with tanned skin and long, glossy black hair stood a few feet in front of her *inside the apartment*. The woman wore a white, flowy garment that looked ancient, but that wasn't the strangest thing about her.

The strangest thing was that she was glowing and partially transparent. Her beautiful face crinkled into a sneer, then she flickered and vanished.

Amy's heart hammered in her chest. Her breath came out in ragged gasps, and she found herself slumping to the ground in the entrance, not noticing the coldness of the tile beneath her. She shook for several minutes before she closed the door. Putting her back against the cold door, she hugged her knees to her chest.

What was that?!

"I think you mean, who was that?" A thunderous female voice rang through her head, and Amy cried out and clasped her hands over her ears, looking around with wide, terrified eyes, but no one was there. *"No one is here, you stupid girl. I am within you."*

Amy stood up jerkily and flung her backpack to the ground, looking around wildly. She could hear her heart in her ears while somehow also feeling it in her throat.

"Who are you? *Where* are you?!" she croaked. The lamp on the table beside the front door shook, and her chest was tight from her gasping lungs. Tears pricked her eyes.

"Are you always this dense? I cannot believe you are a descendent of Anna."

"Wh-what do you mean? Who's Anna?"

The voice sighed. *"You have noticed changes since the morning of your sixteenth birthday, yes?"* Amy stared unseeingly at the floor, memories of the last few days slamming through her mind. The lamp shuddered harder.

"Are you doing that?" she demanded, voice shaking as her eyes shot again to the lamp.

"No, you are." The voice no longer boomed, but it still held power in every syllable.

As her terror reached a crescendo, light burst from her chest and flowed from her, pushing everything away and creating a perfect, golden sphere around her now floating body. A sense of rightness rushed through her, replacing the fear, and she closed her eyes, basking in the euphoria of this light. It was as if every cell in her body was at peace, and her very soul was warm and free.

"What's happening to me?" Amy asked, her hands coming together in front of her chest as if praying, her arms moving instinctively. The bubble around her popped, and she crashed to the ground, pain searing up from her tailbone. She heard a muffled shout of "Keep it down up there!" coming from downstairs and ignored it.

There was another sigh in her mind as the voice spoke within her. "*You do not need to speak out loud to commune with me.*"

She stared around, her mind and heart racing again. The euphoria was gone. "That's it. I've gone crazy."

"*You are not insane, you are manifesting your powers.*"

"That's what a voice I made up would say." A tendril of golden light wound out from her body and split into two parts. Amy stared at it, mouth hanging open. It shot back at her and pinched her arm. Yelping, she jumped back. The pain was very real.

"*As you can see, you are not dreaming.*" The voice sounded amused. "*About eight generations ago, your ancestor, Anna Jones, was a host for me, the Shield. She battled with the Sword of Darkness and banished it back to the nothingness from whence it came. However, the spirit of the Sword of Darkness walks the earth once again, so I have been reborn through you. It is your duty as the reborn Shield of Light to battle the Sword of Darkness, lest it destroy us all.*"

Amy vaguely recognized Anna's name from the time when Arty got really into genealogy. The spirit listened to her memories and then resumed.

"When life and light were first created from the nothingness of darkness, the darkness was displeased. It reviled the noise and chaos of light and, in its spite, created the Sword of Darkness. The purpose of the Sword is to destroy life and bring quiet back to the universe." Amy's brain felt like it was moving through molasses, and she couldn't respond.

The spirit continued. *"In an act of self-defense, the Shield of Light was born from the universe—I was born to defend against the Sword. For millennia, the Sword and I have fought. The Earth became populated with sentient life before any other planet, which drew the Sword to it.*

Eventually, we became so weak that we had to possess living beings to do battle. When humanity evolved, we found you creatures to be the ideal vessels. Every few centuries, we are reborn into the bloodlines of the original humans we possessed. So far, I have won every battle, though the recovery time between each battle becomes longer as we grow weaker."

Coldness swept over Amy, and she started to shake.

This could not be happening.

This wasn't *real*. Her very soul cried out with the truth of the spirit's words, and her shaking increased.

"The Sword of Darkness is back, and, a year after its return, you were born with me inside of you. I have slept inside you and protected you from harm. I saved you from the accident that killed your parents. I woke up that night, but only long enough to save you. I don't experience emotions like humans, but I do regret not being able to spare you the pain of becoming an orphan."

Amy stared at the ground, her eyes wide. "What..." she finally croaked. "What happens to the hosts? To me?"

"*You might live if we are victorious. So far, I have killed all of the Sword's hosts, but some of mine have died in battle as well.*" The spirit spoke calmly as if this was perfectly normal. Amy's head became light, and her lungs felt like they weren't getting enough air. She stood, wringing her hands.

"So, what you're saying is that I may have to fight to the *death*? That there is a very real chance I'm going to—that I'm going to—" Her breaths began to come in gasps and dizziness swamped her. She staggered to the living room, belatedly recognizing the panic attack taking over. Hot tears coursed down her face as she gave into the first full attack she'd had in ages.

An almost stretching sensation surfaced within her, and suddenly, she was off the ground with a golden bubble of light formed around her, pushing everything away from her again. She flailed frantically in the air and heard the spirit within her sigh again.

"*I am part of you. My power, our power, responds to your emotions and will always try to protect you. Right now, there is nothing to protect you from, so I would appreciate it if you would stop.*"

"Oh thanks, that's really helpful," Amy snapped. "Stop panicking? My anxiety is cured."

"*Humans confound me. Anna was never like this, she was ready for adventure. I found her to be a very agreeable host.*"

"Good for Anna!" Amy half yelled, trying her best not to draw any more attention from the neighbors. "I'm not Anna, and I don't want whatever *this*," she gestured around her, "is." Rage began to override her anxiety. The bubble popped the instant she switched emotional gears, and she crashed to the ground. Groaning, she struggled to rise.

"Like it or not, stupid girl, you are my host. Together we are the Shield, and you will train to fight the Sword, and you will save the world. I have not battled for my entire existence and grieved the lives of countless hosts just for one foolish girl to ruin everything." Amy felt the presence of the spirit vanish, like it had gone to sleep.

She staggered to her feet and quickly cleaned up. Then she went and passed out in her bed, instantly. She didn't even feel it when she hit the covers.

S HE WAS AWAKENED LATER BY ARTY GENTLY SHAKing her shoulder. "Hey, Ames, you feeling okay? You've been asleep since I got home."

She moaned and clutched her head, her thoughts spinning out of control. "No, I think I'm sick. Can I stay home tomorrow?" Arty gave her a worried look, got up, and came back with the thermometer.

"You don't have a fever," he said as he read the display. "But you look terrible."

"Thanks, just what every girl wants to hear."

Arty laughed. "You can stay home. I'll get you some water, then you should probably go back to sleep. You hungry?"

"Not even a little. Can you call the school in the morning and see if you can get my homework sent over? I don't want to fall behind."

"Okay. But I'm going to make you eat breakfast tomorrow." She nodded and he left. She took a second to give Satomi and Adam each a heads up that she'd be out sick the next day.

Curling up under the covers, she buried her face in her pillow and sobbed.

6

Amy

AMY'S TEMPLES THROBBED. HER EYES WOULD barely open, so she patted her bedside table to find her phone. She almost fell out of bed reaching for it but managed to grab it and click the screen on, cracking open one eye to check the time.

"Noon?!" she yelped, leaping to her feet. She crumpled to the ground, her head simultaneously heavy and light. She clutched her temples and breathed deeply. It took her a few moments, but the events of last night slowly trickled back into her waking mind.

Moaning, she lay down on the ground and shut her eyes tightly. She was acutely aware of something swirling in her chest, and assumed it was the Shield she'd been feeling all along. Thinking back, it felt surreal, like it had happened to someone else, but the truth rang deep in her soul. It felt right. She felt... whole. The thought scared her.

Arty barged into the room. "Amy, are you okay?!" He placed a hand on her forehead. "You still don't have a fever. What happened?"

"I feel better than last night, but my head still hurts. I think I stood up too quickly." Arty frowned.

"Let's get you back into bed, and I'll get you some water. You hungry?" Arty helped her up. Her stomach growled as she settled in. "Apparently you are. What sounds good?"

"Vicodin." Arty laughed. She wasn't sure she wanted to tell Arty what had happened, it sounded too crazy.

"I'll see what I can do," he replied, pulling the blanket up under her chin.

Amy checked her phone.

Satomi: I hope you get well soon! I MISS YOU SOOO MUCH! 😭😭😭

Adam: Hey, just wanted to check in to see how you're feeling. Get better bestie.

Amy closed her eyes. *That's the Adam I know. Why can't he be like that with everyone?* The pain had already started to lessen by the time Arty came back with a plate of pancakes and a big cup of water, the smell of maple syrup making her mouth water. The water was a welcome balm before she devoured the pancakes with gusto, barely tasting them. The minute the sugar hit her stomach, she felt better. She moved the dishes to the side of her bed.

"Thanks," she said. "That helped. I'm gonna take a shower and then do homework. Were you able to get it?"

"Being friends with your homeroom teacher certainly has its advantages," he replied. "Vanessa got the information from your other teachers and told you to take it easy."

"Thanks," Amy said as she walked to the bathroom.

A NYTHING IN PARTICULAR YOU WANT FOR DINner? We could watch a movie if you're done with your homework," Arty said.

"I'm up for anything," she said. "Having the whole day to work put me ahead."

The spirit's voice echoed in Amy's head. "*If you have time to lollygag with your brother, you have time to start training.*"

It took every ounce of Amy's willpower not to jump, scream, or react visibly. She told Arty that she needed a break from sci-fi before excusing herself to the bathroom. She turned on the bathroom light and fan, then closed the door behind her before mentally rounding on the spirit.

"*Excuse me, freeloader, but I don't have time for you right now. I acknowledge your existence and that I need to train, I can feel that much is true. But I have a life, and you do not get to interrupt it or tell me what to do. If I don't die, I need to get into Clearwater and that means I need time to be normal. We can figure out when to fit training in later.*"

The spirit let out a long, suffering sigh. "*Do you not understand what is at stake?*" Her words were tinged with disgust.

Amy clenched her fists, relishing the feeling of her nails pressing painfully into her skin. The sensation grounded her enough to keep from screaming. "*I do understand what's at stake. I also didn't ask for any of this. I didn't ask to have to fight, I didn't ask to have to kill someone or die trying, and I sure as heck didn't ask for power.*" Anger burned in her and as it did, a little burst of golden light shot out and zapped a bathroom tile, cracking it. She gaped at it.

She felt the spirit's smugness. "*The first step toward controlling your power is controlling yourself. As you recall, your powers are tied to your emotions. Having emotions is normal and feeling them is normal, but you are not normal. We are the Shield, and with that title and destiny comes a great deal of power and responsibility. You need to train, you do not have time for normal.*" Amy could almost hear Arty saying, "With great power comes great responsibility." "*You will start with meditation and learning to control your little... outbursts.*"

Amy ground her teeth together to keep from replying out loud. "*We will start when I say we start. I may not be normal, but this is still my life.*" When the spirit didn't reply, Amy flushed the toilet and washed her hands, grumbling to herself about jerk spirits.

"*I heard that.*"

"*You were supposed to.*"

<hr>

AFTER DINNER AND A LIGHT-HEARTED COMEDY, Amy was finally able to lock herself in her room, the smile she'd plastered on all evening sliding off as she walked in and closed the door. She could feel that the spirit was "awake." She wasn't sure how she knew what that felt like and didn't think about it too hard. "Alright, Spirit. Let's do this. Where do we start?" she asked in a quiet voice.

The spirit wasted no time. "*Take a seat. Many humans find it easier to meditate while on a firm surface, I have found.*" Amy sat cross-legged in the center of her room after grabbing a pillow from her bed to sit on, shifting uncomfortably as she waited for the next instruction. "*Close your eyes. You may be able to meditate with your eyes open but closing them makes it easier to drive out distractions.*" Sitting up straighter, she placed her hands in her lap and closed her eyes. "*Breathe in for a count of four, hold your breath for a count of four and then release for a count of four. Focus on the feeling of breathing, like how the air feels entering and exiting your body.*"

Breathing as instructed, her body relaxed, and her heart rate slowed slightly. She focused on the coldness of the air moving into her nose and the warmth as it left her.

"*As the breathing becomes more automatic, notice the feeling of sitting on the floor. Feel the fabric against your skin from your clothes. Let everything in while focusing on nothing in particular.*"

Amy's eye twitched slightly. It felt like she was going to explode just sitting there. Her knee bounced.

After a few confused minutes, a spark of light shot from her body toward her bed. Her eyes popped open as the scent of burning hit her, and she bolted to quickly pat the spark out, feeling very little heat.

Great. She loved that comforter and now it was singed.

"*You are not listening,*" the spirit said.

Amy rolled her eyes.

Wrestling her temper, which seemed stronger as of late, she attempted to send the feeling of a glare at the spirit in her mind. Being in her head for her art had made it a lot easier than she anticipated. "What you're saying doesn't make any sense. How do I focus on everything *and* nothing?" She resumed her spot on the floor. "After this session, we should probably move these outside."

"*The purpose of meditation is to clear your mind and, in your case, to be better able to control your emotions.*"

"Fine, but like, don't people usually listen to some kind of music or something when they meditate?"

The spirit paused. "*Perhaps they do in this time, but I am not familiar with that practice.*"

"I usually listen to music when I paint or draw, and that's about as close as I get to having a clear mind."

The spirit seemed deep in thought for a few moments before abruptly saying, "*Get your sketchbook. I would like to monitor you while you create.*"

Amy grabbed a sketchbook from a stack, went to sit at her desk, and took out her pencils. She put her headphones on and played some calming, instrumental music.

For several minutes, she stared blankly at the paper, the pencil not moving.

"*Problem?*"

"I'm not used to being watched while I work, sorry," she replied sarcastically. "I'm having trouble thinking of what to draw."

The spirit said nothing in response, so Amy went back to staring at the blank page. After a few minutes, her mind opened, and a tidal wave of ideas flowed through her. She felt the most like herself, the most alive, when she was creating. It was as if she were in her own world. She put pencil to paper and sketched, her mind clearing. The only things she thought of were the images in her mind and how to best get it on paper.

After half an hour had passed, a sketch of her favorite entrance to Whittaker Hills Park was before her. She tried to recall as many minute details as she could to bring the picture to life. She blinked, breaking herself out of her reverie.

"Acceptable job. This method, though somewhat unconventional, might work best for you. But we still need to determine a method for you to take this peace with you wherever you go."

"Does the Sword's host train too?" Her thoughts had been drawn to this mystery person a lot more than she liked. She couldn't eat animals, how could she be expected to kill someone? Her stomach churned as her thoughts got carried away.

"Yes. The Sword's host is supported by a society called the Sheath. They are committed to the Sword and worship it as if it were a god and support the family of the original host. During the intervening centuries between incarnations, they do their best to sew discord and destruction and to gain power so as to better support the Sword, even at the cost of their lives. They're all sycophants who either want power or were raised to blindly follow their doctrine."

"Do you know who the Sword is?"

"No, I have been asleep for almost two hundred years. I am sure they will make themselves known to you soon. Generally, once we awaken, there is a shall we say, waiting period

while we both try to train our hosts and rebuild our power. The Sword's host will have an advantage, as they've probably been training since they were born." Amy gulped, feeling cold sweat break out across her forehead.

"Training since birth?" Nausea crawled up her throat. Sparks lit her eyes as she tried to control her breathing.

The spirit continued, barely acknowledging her. *"The Sword's line has been revered for centuries, and it enjoys the wealth and adoration of its host's family. They train every child until they reach the age of eighteen in case they are chosen. Their children are always ready to strike at my host as soon as the time is ripe."*

Amy was silent, absorbing everything as a chill spread from her chest outwards.

The spirit paused briefly. *"Your family, however, has never been worshipped. The secret of the Shield, of me, is sometimes told from parent to child through the generations, though every now and again, a generation is lost. You are one such generation."*

Did my parents know? Did my parents know that I was going to have to train and fight and maybe even... kill someone? She tried to think back, her memories of them hazy, but she would remember being told something like this. Her breathing started to come out in sharp gasps, and she felt dizzy. Her ears buzzed.

I can't do this. I can't fight someone. I can't... kill someone. I can't... I can't...

All at once, a gold light expanded outward from her into a perfect sphere, and her mouth opened in a scream as her head fell back. To someone outside the bubble, the scream would have appeared silent. However, in Amy's unprotected ears, it was a loud, gut-wrenching sound dripping with fear and agony. Terror beat through every cell in her body, overwhelming her. Her arms stretched out wide behind her, the scream seemingly unending. The sphere was tight and swirling around her.

She collapsed back to the ground, unconscious, the light cushioning her fall.

7

Amy

ALL SHIFTED INTO WINTER. AFTER BEING ABLE to control her emotions better and meditate with ease, the spirit decided Amy was ready to move on to the next phase of training: intentionally using her power. Amy couldn't decide if she was excited or terrified by this change.

As she wandered into a secluded part of the park, the familiar smells of the evergreen trees and nature did nothing to assuage her nerves. She went to a small field hidden deep in the woods that surrounded the park, an unmaintained area where no one generally went.

"The first thing we will start with is consciously creating a bubble of energy around yourself, akin to what you have done unconsciously before. We, the Shield, are first and foremost a shield after all." Amy caught the ghost of humor in the spir-

it's voice, and she smiled despite herself. *"Close your eyes and find me within you. Breathe as you have practiced."*

Amy inhaled deeply. She hadn't tried to "touch" the spirit yet. The voice in her head and the feeling in her body were connected, she knew, but they felt separate. She mentally reached into her chest and grasped at the presence that never left her. Her breath caught in her throat. It was overwhelming, like it could shove her aside and drive her body without consent. Her breathing became rapid.

"Amy, let go!" the spirit commanded. For a moment, she was held by the raw power inside of her. Impressions and images she couldn't comprehend rushed through her mind. A sense of pure, unbridled power and flashes of light overwhelmed her. She stopped breathing, and the flashes intensified.

The world went black.

*H*OW ARE YOU FEELING?*"*
There was a large rock digging painfully into her back, and the grass was a little too damp, water seeping into her clothes. She sat up, holding her head. "How long was I out?"

"Not even a full minute. Sometimes, when a host first makes direct contact with me, my power and age overwhelm them. They react in several ways, but losing consciousness is one of the most common."

"Oh, good. I'd hate to be the only one to pass out," Amy said sarcastically, rolling her eyes.

"*Are you able to try again?*" The spirit rarely responded to humor or sarcasm.

"Sure." Amy stood with a bit of effort and resumed her stance, breathing steadily and closing her eyes, allowing herself to relax. Once her mind was clear, she tentatively reached into herself again. The presence was warm in the center of her chest. The power responded in a more subdued manner, whispering to her and brushing delicately against her consciousness. *Maybe the spirit was the problem and not me.*

"*Now take the power, pull it out, and shape it.*"

Amy mentally pulled at the power. Nothing happened.

She imagined a pot full of shimmering, golden paint, imagining the power within her as the paint. Envisioning a paintbrush, she dipped it into the paint, swirling the golden contents. The paint shimmered and glowed with untapped potential. Pulling the paintbrush out in her mind, she moved her hand as if starting to paint. There was a tug through her and then warmth. She painted a perfect orb with the brush, broad strokes creating the image in her mind.

Opening her eyes, she found herself floating in the air surrounded by a bubble of softly glowing, golden light. A bubble just like the one she'd painted in her mind. Forgetting herself, a spike of elation raced through her. The power reveled in her joy, and the soft glow became a vibrant, almost searing white. There was a fierce sort of happiness from the spirit at her acceptance of it. It was the first sensation close to an emotion Amy had felt come from her, other than frustration. A song of exultation sang through her soul, and she held her hands aloft, barely holding back from singing herself.

Amy peered out from her sphere and saw that the sky was beginning to grow dark. With a sigh, she released the power. She had been created and born for the sole purpose of possessing this power, and, while her mind might be absolutely terrified, her body felt the rightness of it. She floated to the ground as the light receded.

"Excellent work. We appear to have a more natural bond than previous hosts. We are done for the night."

Amy meandered down a path at random, as was her habit. This time to herself kept her grounded. The park was one of her favorite places in the world, and she knew it well. Her shoulders relaxed as she breathed in the scent of pine trees. It was pure bliss. Suddenly, her power recoiled inside of her, startling her.

"So, you're the Shield," an icy voice said behind her. Amy whirled to see a boy about her age leaning against a tree. "I felt you from across the park." His emerald eyes were piercing, and she felt like they were blazing a hole straight through to her core. The spirit swirled aggressively inside of her, the joy from earlier melting away completely.

8

Amy

AMY STOOD HER GROUND, LOOKING HIM IN THE eye despite her insides feeling like they were shaking. Her senses, or more likely, the spirit's senses, were screaming that this was her enemy.

"And... you are?" she responded in the snottiest tone she could muster as she jutted a hip out. She was immensely proud that her voice hadn't shaken, and her gaze hadn't wavered.

"I am the Sword's host," he replied, his tone urbane. Her outfit seemed frumpy and out of place compared to his dark, clearly tailored clothes. He stood casually as if he hadn't a care in the world.

She crossed her arms over her chest and made a show of slowly looking him up and down, her lips pursed and her expression unimpressed. He seemed familiar, but she couldn't place him. Amy's shyness flared, but she squashed it. She wasn't going to let this creep scare her... even if he kind of did.

In a show of haughty bravery that she didn't feel, she stepped toward him and leaned in. "Is that supposed to impress me?" She was almost close enough to feel his breath on her, but didn't move away, although every nerve in her body begged her to.

He looked slightly taken aback as his smirk dropped and his eyes widened. Amy almost laughed, but held it in. He leaned away ever so slightly. *Not so tough now, are you?*

"Be impressed or not, it doesn't matter to me. I'm here to tell you that I am going to be the final Sword—the Sword that breaks the Shield." He placed a fingertip under her chin, forcing her head slightly further back. She didn't flinch.

"Is that so?" she asked, a smile lighting up her face. She watched in satisfaction as confusion flitted across his face at her sudden change in demeanor. *Ha, he's as uptight as I thought.* "Say, do I know you?" she asked, the haughty façade dropping entirely. She rarely forgot a pretty color and those green eyes were very familiar.

"Of course you do. We go to the same high school, there's only one in the area," he said, running a hand through his hair. "If there were a private institution around, I would go there. You are Amy Sanders. You're a sophomore in Mrs. Sanchez's homeroom." Amy struggled to keep her face from changing expressions at this information. "And you rudely ran into me in the hallway once, remember?" She fought a blush.

"You know all that about me, why not tell me about yourself? If we're destined to kill each other, we should at least be on a first-name basis." The faint bitterness in her voice couldn't be missed.

His shoulders slumped and he ran a hand through his hair again. "You are the Shield, and I am the Sword. We're enemies."

"Says who?" Amy asked. She stepped back, allowing the boy some room to breathe. "I only recently learned about this whole Shield and Sword thing," she admitted. He blew out a breath. "Are you a freshman?" she asked, her lips twitching with a suppressed smile. This boy was easy to fluster, and she was overcome by an impish desire to frazzle him. His cheeks reddened ever so slightly.

"No, of course not," he retorted hotly. "I'm a junior. My name is Connor Callaghan." He bowed somewhat graciously, the aristocratic air about him coming to light. He was clearly from the upper class, so clearly not originally from Whittaker Hills. She stuck her hand out, and Connor stared at it.

"Bowing is so last century," she said with a wink. Connor had the ghost of a smile on his face as he straightened up and took her hand. A jolt shot up her arm as the spirits inside them recoiled from each other. The sensation of electricity ripped through Amy, burning her insides. They leapt back, breathing hard. "Well," she managed to say. "Perhaps we should avoid that."

Connor gave a half smile. "Perhaps," he agreed, not looking away, and his eyes went cold again. "The spirits have hated each other since long before man came into being." He dropped his arms to his sides. "That is our destiny."

"If you say so," she replied, then tossed her hair behind her shoulders with a shake of her head. She returned his cold stare with a warm one. "I don't have any reason to hate you or want to kill you."

"Yet," he responded before turning his back on her and walking away.

9

Connor

As Connor walked out of the woods and onto a path, he was suddenly flanked by men wearing dark suits. They seemed to appear out from the shadows as they walked a step behind him. "What was the Shield host like, Mr. Connor?" one asked deferentially.

"Strange. She's a strange girl," Connor answered, rubbing his chin.

"Strange?"

"Yes, strange," he snapped, turning to glare. "Don't repeat my words." The man flinched. Connor lapsed into a pensive silence as he made his way to the park entrance he had come through. The other host was not at all what he'd been expecting. The wind whistled through the trees, and the shadows seemed to darken when Connor walked by. He paid them no mind—darkness always responded to the spirit within him.

They made it to the end of the path, and he hadn't spoken the entire time. One of the men ran ahead to open a rear door of a sleek black Mercedes, and Connor stepped in without acknowledging him. After closing the door, the men got into the front seats and drove toward Whittaker Estates. The closer the car got to his home, the more his stomach started to twist as it always did at the thought of speaking to his father. He moderated his expression and his body's movements to hide the pangs of anxiety.

The car stopped outside the third gate from the main road. The driver pressed a button outside the gate, and after a moment of waiting, the imposing black gate slid open and they drove up the long, winding driveway. The yard was pristine, and the outside of the dark gray house was immaculate and in perfect repair.

⎯⎯⎯⎯⎯

WERE YOU ABLE TO INITIATE CONTACT WITH the Shield?" Connor's father, Preston, demanded as soon as Connor entered the parlor. He was a tall, slender man with dark hair.

"Yes, sir," Connor answered automatically, standing as straight as possible. He worked hard to keep from looking away from his father's green eyes, the same shade as his own. Eye contact was a newly bestowed honor he wasn't yet accustomed to.

"Excellent work, host. Tell us what happened."

Connor summarized the meeting in the park, leaving out any of his emotional responses. Connor's mother,

Catherine, sipped tea throughout the conversation, clearly caring very little for the details. "The Shield is inhabiting a very strange girl," he concluded. His father scoffed.

"She sounds like a weak and naïve little girl," his father sneered as Catherine casually examined her nails, staying silent. Her blonde hair was perfectly coifed, not a strand out of place. She'd never been one to look or act motherly. Connor looked back at his father as he continued speaking. "Try to gain her confidence to throw her off balance and then kill her when the Sword decides the time is right. Becoming her friend will cause such a stupid, silly girl to drop her guard and make the final battle easier for us."

"It'll be difficult, as the Sword's hatred of her sways my actions at times," Connor said. His father's eyes narrowed. "But I *will* succeed Father," he said, bowing his head. When Connor sensed his father's dismissal, he left the sitting room and went to his bedroom, throwing himself gracelessly onto his bed. Thoughts of Amy's infuriating smile and sparkling eyes enraged him. *What's there to smile about?*

10

Amy

A FEW DAYS LATER, AMY WENT BACK TO THE park, though not for training. Having hit a block with a project for art class, she wandered around looking for inspiration. She inhaled deeply, relishing the smells of the evergreen trees mixing with the loam beneath them. The crisp air against her skin was rejuvenating.

A burst of joy coursed through her when she came upon the empty swings. As she swung, images of abstract bursts of vibrant colors played through her mind, as well as potential stills of an empty park. How could she convey happiness through an empty park, which would otherwise look lonely? *Perhaps in the lighting? Maybe the colors.* She settled into a rhythm of swinging.

Her reverie was broken when she felt a stirring in her chest that had her immediate attention. Jumping off the swing, she froze and faced where her senses pointed. Connor strode into view, a smirk on his face. He walked onto the playground as if that was his destination all along. They made eye contact and for a moment, neither spoke.

"I guess the park's ruined for me," Connor said, sneering. Amy smiled wide.

"Good afternoon, Connor," she said with a chuckle, walking to within a few feet of her mortal enemy. "You like to come here to wander too?"

"I don't see how what I do is any of your business."

She laughed. "Fine, be rude."

"We are *enemies*!" he exploded. "You had to have felt the Shield respond to me."

"Yeah, but I'm not 'the Shield,' and you're not 'the Sword,' not really. They're parasites that are using us." Contempt and disgust dripped from her words. She thought that Connor, more than anyone, would understand her conflicted feelings toward the spirit.

"Parasites!" he exclaimed. "It is a great honor to be a vessel for the Sword." Her eyebrows shot up.

"I apologize, I'd forgotten you were raised in a cult." Amy's smile dropped and Connor's face flushed. After a few minutes of tense silence, she finally sighed and spoke. "If you're done being petulant, you can leave. I was here first."

His glare turned into a look of disbelief and then he threw his head back and laughed, loud and long. Amy tilted her head to the side, confusion plain on her face. He laughed until he was clutching at his sides and doubled over. "No one..." He gasped. "Has ever spoken to me like that." He straightened, wiping his eyes, an actual smile on his face. Amy was silent, completely taken aback. Her cheeks burned lightly as she took in his smile. His stunning smile.

"No one's ever called you on your BS before?"

"My... BS?"

"Yeah. You can believe whatever you want, but these spirits are using us. We're vessels for them to use to fight each other. They only protect us to protect themselves."

"It's a great honor to be chosen to serve one of the spirits. Only two people every few centuries are chosen, we are special. Surely, you feel the rightness of the union in your soul."

Amy shifted uncomfortably. "If you say so," she said. The fight didn't seem worth it. "Regardless, if we're enemies, why not attack me now?" Comparing their sizes, she really didn't want him to. She imagined that growing up in his cult, or whatever, he had been taught a lot more than she had.

Connor looked at her in disbelief. "Do you not know anything?" he asked. "The spirits decide when our battle takes place. They will not allow us to randomly attack each other."

"Oh," she replied, wincing. "Sorry, I wasn't indoctrinated." Her tone became scornful.

"I'd heard that the Shield spirit does things a bit differently than the Sheath," he conceded.

"I guess so."

Connor's hands twitched slightly, but he stood ramrod straight. They looked at each other for a long, drawn-out moment, not breaking eye contact. Amy wasn't sure what he saw, but she thought she saw his expression soften, but it quickly turned back to a sneer.

"The Shield spirit has obviously degenerated over the centuries. Just look at you." Amy raised an eyebrow at him.

"You are *nothing* compared to me. I have trained my whole life for this, and you? You're scrawny and ignorant." His eyes narrowed.

Amy almost laughed. No one had ever called her scrawny. Perhaps he'd meant weak? Brushing off her amusement, she put a fist on her hip. "At least I had a life before this crap started. What did you have? Fancy things and training? We might die, but I'd rather have my memories than all the training in the world." His face paled, then went scarlet.

Connor shot a spear of gray light at her, stopping it inches from her face. The cold slap of air from its flight hit her, and it was like ice spreading into her limbs as goose bumps erupted across her body. The power within her expanded outward, throwing a golden sphere around her.

"You know nothing, you stupid girl," he spat, arms trembling as if he was fighting to move the spear closer to her. "It's an honor to lead the life I have led in the service of the Sword."

Amy's face broke into what could only be called a snarl, magma replacing the ice. "You pathetic, sad little boy, you don't even know what a real life is. You don't know what it means to be a real person." Connor's eyes filled with an almost palpable hate. The glow around her expanded further, stopping short of him and throwing his spear aside.

Power crackled in the air. Connor stood down first, exhaling a breath and recalling his energy. "I guess you have a reason to hate me now," he said.

She considered that. "I don't hate you," she replied, withdrawing her power and settling back onto the ground.

"You're too naïve to be the Shield. I think you really will be the first Shield to break."

She shrugged at his words, still feeling the burning anger inside her. There was a tinge of sadness for this poor, deluded boy within the burn. "We'll see, silly little Swordling."

Connor huffed and stomped out of sight. *So much for his dignified act.* Amy dropped onto the grass shaking once she felt he was gone. Her breath was coming out in pants and her limbs trembled as she curled her knees into her chest. *I've never been so angry, so often, before. Is this because of the Shield?*

11

Amy

ON ONE PARTICULARLY BEAUTIFUL DAY TWO months later, after her daily weightlifting and cardio, Amy wandered through the park again. She didn't have as much free time anymore and relished this opportunity to do nothing. She walked the familiar trails and closed her eyes in contentment, following the path she was on by memory. Her phone dinged.

Amy grimaced, staring at the message, unsure of how to reply. *I miss you too, Satomi. But–*

"OOF!" she exclaimed as she slammed into something hard. Everything blurred. A pair of strong hands caught her upper arms, clutching her tightly, but not enough to hurt. She steadied herself and looked up into a pair of surprised emerald eyes. The Shield within her flared, but Amy suppressed it, having gained some mastery over herself. Connor let go of her, and for the briefest of moments, their eyes locked. He seemed transfixed before he practically pushed her away. Flailing, she righted herself before she could hit the wet ground.

"What kind of surprise attack was that?" he mocked, aggressively running a hand through his hair. Amy couldn't help herself, she looked at the ground as her cheeks burned. "What a crap Shield you are."

A haze of red descended over her vision. *Months of work, effort, pain, loneliness... and he's making fun of me?!*

For the first time in her entire life, a snapping sensation echoed from deep inside of her, and her arm shot out as she tried to punch him in the face. He caught her fist and held it, not retaliating. They made eye contact again, green and blue eyes lost in each other. In a moment, she came back to herself and jumped back, horrified.

Without thinking, she stuttered, "I am *so* sorry!" while covering her mouth with her hands. Connor continued to stare at her. She stepped back and put her arms behind her. She felt the sting of tears in her eyes.

"You're... sorry?" he asked, tilting his head to the side.

"Yes!" she shouted somewhat frantically. "I am so, *so* sorry! I've never hit anyone before. I don't know what came over me!"

Connor started to laugh. "You really don't know anything, do you?" he asked. This time, he didn't say it cruelly. "The spirit inside of you can affect your mood. You may not normally be an angry person, but when you're with me, you are not merely you anymore—you are the Shield, and you will have its prejudices. It also dulls anxieties around your fate." It was Amy's turn to stare. That certainly explained why she'd been so chill with everything. She'd thought it was shock and had been waiting for it to wear off.

"I thought you hated me and were my mortal enemy." She grinned. "Why are you explaining things to me?"

"Because stupidity offends me."

She laughed. She felt the fire inside her try to reignite, but this time she suppressed it with mirth. "I think the right word here would be ignorance. I may not be the smartest person in the world, but I wouldn't say I'm stupid."

"If you say so," he responded, running his hand through his hair again.

"So... come here often?" Amy could punch herself. It sounded like a cheesy pickup line. She cleared her throat.

"Uh...I guess?"

"I uh, didn't mean for that to sound so... so weird," she muttered.

"I guess I do come here often," he answered slowly. "There isn't really much else to do in this tiny town."

"Whittaker Hills isn't that bad," she admonished. "I love this place."

"You do?"

"Yeah! This park is my favorite place in the entire world." Her face glowed as she talked about it. "I come here a lot to think or to get inspiration."

"Inspiration?"

"Yeah, for a project."

"What kind of project?"

"A little hobby of mine." She skirted the subject. "What do you like to do?" Connor hesitated.

"I train in a few forms of martial arts and study some extracurriculars." Amy's chest tightened at the mention of his superior training.

"That's pretty cool. Do you enjoy them?"

"I just do what I need to do to be a proper host."

"Oh. Well...um... I gotta get going," Amy said.

"Very well. Next time you are out here, try to watch where you are going."

"Right."

12

Amy

THE NEXT DAY, AMY AND SATOMI WERE SITTING alone at lunch as usual.

"I know it's a long way off, but I can't stop thinking about planning a party for the end of summer, I want to have a big bash. What do you think?" Satomi was bouncing in her seat, which sent bits of food flying everywhere.

"I would love that. We could—" A familiar churning sensation erupted in Amy's middle. She looked around and saw Connor approaching their table. She gaped open-mouthed as he sat down without preamble beside her. Satomi stared, her mouth hanging wide open too.

"Good afternoon, Amy," Connor said, his manners seemingly on full blast.

"Uh, Amy?" Satomi squeaked, rounding on her. "Who is *he*?"

His face remained neutral and pleasant as he looked back at her like he belonged there. Fighting the urge to roll her eyes, she said, "And Connor, this is my best friend Satomi. I've bumped into Connor a few times in the park. He's a bit of a jerk." Amy turned and grinned at her enemy, whose wide eyes met hers before he let out a laugh.

"I suppose 'a bit of a jerk' isn't the worst thing I've been called," he replied urbanely. Amy wasn't sure, but he seemed to be putting on a façade. Satomi blushed as she looked at him, no doubt taking in his handsome face and dignified manner. For the first time in a long time, Amy witnessed Satomi at an utter loss for words. She barely suppressed another grin.

"Well, you're not the worst all the time, but you are pretty terrible." She tossed her hair and shrugged. Amy thought she saw the ghost of a blush color his cheeks. "What do you want? Don't you have other people you can hang out with?" Making sure she angled herself between Connor and Satomi, her eyebrows drew together. *What if he hurts Satomi?*

"Of course I have other people I could sit with, but I thought I'd come and visit you today."

"You did, huh?" she asked suspiciously. "How magnanimous of you." She glanced at Satomi's face, catching her shocked expression.

"Do you take issue with that?" he asked.

"And if I do?"

"I suppose we could duke it out, but I would prefer to just sit here."

"Whatever," Amy said, turning away from him. "So, Satomi, when were you thinking of having your party *that Connor isn't invited to*?" Satomi looked borderline scandalized. A laugh escaped Connor again, but he covered his mouth quickly.

As Connor laughed, Adam walked by but stopped in his tracks upon seeing Connor sitting there. He immediately walked toward them. "Hey, Ames. What's up?" Adam sat his almost empty tray down on the table and smiled at her. He turned and looked at Connor. "Oh hello, I'm Adam Whittaker." Amy suddenly felt new tension in the air.

"Connor Callaghan," he replied with what Amy thought was supposed to be a charming smile. "I believe we're neighbors. You're the house at the end of the main road at Whittaker Estates, yes?"

Adam flinched. "Nice to meet you, neighbor. How do you know Amy?" Amy caught Satomi's attention and rolled her eyes. Surely, she must be able to feel the testosterone in the air too.

"We ran into each other a few times in the park," Amy interjected. She really didn't want her friends to know about her new and unwilling pastime or about the unwelcome parasite within her. "He's decided to become a bigger nuisance." Her tone was snappy, and Connor smirked in response.

"Would you like me to get rid of him?" Adam asked, flexing his muscles slightly. *Oh, if only he knew.* Avoiding looking at Connor's face to see his expression was hard.

"No, it's fine. If he's lonely and wants to hang out with a stranger, let him. He's not hurting anyone."

"Well, alright then." Adam looked uneasily at Connor's

serene face. "Have a good lunch," he said somewhat gruffly as he picked his tray back up and walked toward a table of guys waving at him.

"It was very nice meeting you, Adam," Connor said politely before turning back to Amy. "It was nice seeing you outside the park and meeting your friends. I need to go and finish my lunch. Have a pleasant rest of your day, Amy. Satomi." He nodded at both, got up, and left.

Satomi looked at his back before turning to Amy. "You have all the luck." She groaned and plunked her head onto the table. Amy looked at her blankly.

"Luck?"

"Yes, luck! You sit there and cute boys show up. I mean, Adam is a tool, but Connor seems like an alright guy."

"An 'alright guy?' I think you mean 'giant jerk.'" His words from the other day still rankled her and caused her blood to boil if she thought about it for too long.

"Then why bother with him at all?"

Amy flinched. How could she answer that without giving away their shared secret?

"I'm not really sure," she said at last, somewhat truthfully. As Sword and Shield, they were inexplicably drawn toward and repulsed by each other. "I guess I don't completely hate him," she conceded, at a loss. Satomi looked at her slyly.

"So, if you don't hate him, does that mean you *like* him?" Satomi teased, clapping her hands with exuberance.

"Satomi!" Amy shoved her playfully, almost knocking her over with her new strength. "I barely like him, much less *like* like him."

"He's cute though."

Amy turned to look at the clock to hide her burning cheeks. "It's almost time to go. We should clean up." She glanced around to keep from making eye contact with Satomi and caught Connor's eye from across the room instead. He was sitting at a table with a small group of well-dressed boys who appeared deferential toward him. Apparently, his cult was even in the school. She grimaced at this, feeling a moment of pity, and he cocked his head to the side, quirking up an eyebrow. She blinked quickly and looked away.

Amy and Satomi hurried to art, where Amy set aside her current project and began to aggressively paint a more abstract piece in shades of fire. Satomi glanced over from her sculpture.

"What are you painting?" Satomi asked curiously. "It doesn't look like realism."

"My feelings," she spat out as she added in shades of black and gold. "I don't want to paint on theme today." By the end of the period, she had painted a black circle surrounded with shimmering gold centered in a sea of flames and black lightning. She usually took her time with her paintings, but this one was an emotional dump.

"Wow, that's a lot of feelings," Satomi commented. "Do you want to talk about it?"

"No, I feel better now."

After the final bell rang, Amy went to the bus stop and scrolled through her various social media feeds. A hand landed on her shoulder. Heart in her throat, she spun and looked up to see Connor pulling his hand back with an amused expression. Glancing around, she was thankful that no one was close by to see her reaction.

She smacked his arm away and scowled. "Why won't you leave me alone today?" she demanded, stamping her foot and wondering how he snuck up on her.

"I can't seem to help myself. I came to offer you a ride home in my car, dear enemy." Amy rolled her eyes.

"Why, so you can see where I live and kill me easier? Hard pass."

He said, "When I kill you, it'll be at the Sword's behest, and it'll know where you are regardless of my knowledge or lack thereof."

"Yes, talk about how you're going to kill me. That will definitely get me to get into a car alone with you." Connor grimaced and his cheeks colored slightly.

"Yes, I suppose that wasn't the best approach," he mused.

She couldn't help but giggle at him. "You don't have very good people skills, do you?"

"No one's ever accused me of such a thing before," he said with a trace of a pout. Amy giggled again. "My manners are impeccable."

"Not when you're talking to me." He flinched, his eyes widening. "My bus is here. Um, have a good day?" Amy didn't wait for a reply before leaving. She couldn't tell if she felt relief or a little sad ending the conversation so abruptly.

13

Connor

CONNOR WALKED TO THE FRONT OF THE school where his family's car was waiting for him. His classmates, Peter and Quinton, were dutifully standing beside his usual driver Roland and his sometimes guard, Vincent. Peter was short and chubby with blond hair whereas Quinton was taller with brown hair and pale skin. Both seemed to cringe into themselves as Connor approached. The two older men stood straighter, each having an imposing build that was accentuated by their tailored black suits.

"How was your day, Mister Connor?" the bulkier of the two men asked as they took their seats. The two men sat up front, and the boys sat in the back.

"Fine, Roland," he answered curtly. The atmosphere in the car became chillier once he spoke, a vocal trick he'd learned from his father. Both men, despite being older and larger, kept their expressions neutral.

"Did you have any contact with the Shield girl?" the other inquired.

"Her name is Amy, Vincent. We should probably call the Shield's host by her proper name if I'm to become her... friend." An uncomfortable silence reigned at this statement. Roland shifted in his seat and Peter looked away, scratching his neck. Connor ignored them.

His mind was otherwise occupied with thoughts of Amy. How was he going to get closer to her? Being nice didn't come naturally, and he was struggling with the concept. *Why do I find her to be so infuriating?*

She didn't respond to his usual charms, and she didn't seem to care much about money either, given her lack of attraction to Adam.

Adam was clearly interested in Amy. *Is she interested in him?* She seemed completely oblivious to his feelings. Poor girl, having the "Whittaker prince" interested in her. He'd found the Whittakers to be a snobbish lot that thought very highly of themselves for owning most of a tiny, former mining town. His family could be classified as snobs, he supposed, but they at least had a right to be. No, Adam was nothing.

The car pulled up to the estate and an old, gray-haired man opened Connor's door once it came to a complete stop.

"Welcome home, sir," the old man said with a bow. He kept his eyes downcast and his posture perfect. The bow seemed to be automatic.

"Good afternoon, Bertram," Connor said. His chest warmed at the sight of the old man.

"What would you like for dinner tonight, sir?"

"Surprise me." Bertram's mustache twitched with what Connor assumed was a smile.

"Very good, sir." Bertram opened the front door, and Connor went to his room. His earlier amusement had drained, leaving behind a coldness that permeated his entire body.

14

Amy

AMY PRESSED HER FACE AGAINST THE BUS window's cool glass and turned up her music in her headphones, drowning out the chatter around her. She wasn't even sure what was playing. Connor was so frustrating. First, he was mean and rude, then he was trying to be nice.

What is his deal? Her head bumped into the window as the bus took a turn a little too quickly while pulling up near her apartment. She made her way to the apartment stairs and hurried up to her door.

"*Did you have a run in with the Sword today?*" the spirit asked as she did every day. Amy was never sure when the spirit was "awake" or not.

Amy hesitated, tempted not to say or think anything so as not to have to deal with the million follow-up questions or with the spirit plumbing her memories. The pause had given her away. Replying in her mind, she said, "*Yeah, I saw Connor today. He came to my table at lunch and then offered me a ride home.*"

"*Did you accept?*"

"*Yes, because I'm completely stupid.*"

The spirit ignored her sarcasm as usual. "*Good. The Sword and Sheath are not to be trusted. I wonder why he sought you out and what his plan is...*"

"*Probably to mess with me. Can we hurry up and do whatever training we have to do? I have a ton of homework.*"

"*Do you not think that it is wiser to spend more time on training than on useless schoolwork?*"

"*I'd like to have a life outside of this whole Shield and Sword crap. I want to go to college after it's all over, assuming I don't die, and I need good grades to get in. The best grades.*"

There was a pause. "*That is understandable. Let us make our way to the park. I would like you to try to work on shielding and flying, then firing energy blasts.*"

Amy sighed. It'd be another night with a headache, just what she and her slightly slipping grades needed.

"I'm home!" Arty called.

"Hey, Arty, you're home early," Amy replied with forced energy and cheer, going to give him a hug. "Have a training run today?"

"Yep! I assume you want to go to the park? If you wait a minute, I'll take you."

Amy waited and they loaded into the car. After they parked, Arty began his run and Amy made her way to the wild outskirts. An hour later, she was sprawled out on the ground, panting and wiping sweat off her face. The grass poked her back uncomfortably, and her lungs burned.

"You are still not sending out enough power."

Amy rolled her eyes.

"I'm trying, but it doesn't feel right. It feels like I'm shooting myself and the trees at the same time." Shielding, bending the power, and flying came easily to her and filled her soul with ecstasy. Attacking and destroying did not.

"We are done for the day. You appear overexerted." Relief washed over Amy at this statement, and she closed her eyes as the spirit's presence faded within her mind.

"Done already?" came a voice from behind her. She jumped up, turning, to see Connor leaning against a partially destroyed tree, wearing what appeared to be designer workout clothes.

"What're you doing here?" she snapped, fixing her hair and brushing grass off her clothes. "Are you stalking me?"

"No." Connor scoffed. "I sensed the Shield and thought I'd come and check out my competition." Amy rolled her eyes.

"Have you been here the *whole* time?" she asked, fidgeting with the hem of her shirt.

"Not the whole time, no."

"Why didn't I sense you?"

"I can mask my power. Are you not able to yet?" Amy ignored him. "You're not very good at this, are you?" Her face turned crimson, and she continued to ignore him, stretching. "Here," he said, holding out his hand and forming a black orb. Amy jumped back and formed a golden Shield around herself. Connor didn't move. "Try focusing your energy into more of a ball rather than the bolts you were doing. That should be easier for you." She blinked and the field around her wavered slightly. The spirit inside of her flared, but she shoved it down without thinking.

"What're you up to?" she asked warily. He extinguished the orb, and she dropped her shield.

Connor's mouth popped open for a moment before he shut it again with a snap, his eyebrows drawing together. "As I said before, stupidity offends me." Amy shook out her tense shoulders and walked over to sit against a tree, trying to hide how exhausted she was. She crossed her legs in front of her and rested her head against the rough bark. Sighing, she ran her hands up her face.

"Why do you keep messing with me? You bug me at school, and you're always at the park. What're you trying to do? What's your deal?" She didn't have the energy for subterfuge.

Hesitating, Connor walked over and gracefully sat at the base of a tree about two feet away from her.

"I find you amusing," he said at last.

"Amusing?" she asked, glancing at him with a raised eyebrow. "Don't you have anything better to do?"

"I guess not."

"Don't you hang out with your friends at all? Those guys I saw you with?" Connor leaned his head back against the tree and looked up at the sky.

"I don't really have 'friends.' I have lackeys and servants, but I'm not 'friends' with them. They are there to do a job."

"That's really sad," Amy said, her face contorting. "Why not?"

Connor was quiet, seeming to watch a particularly fluffy gray cloud float across the darkening sky. "I am the Sword host. My duty is too important for me to waste time on things like that. Most of my free time goes toward studying or training. I am supposed to be running right now." He smiled conspiratorially at her.

"And yet, here you are, sitting with your sworn enemy."

"Here I am." They were silent.

"Can I ask you a random question?" Amy said.

Connor stared at her. "If you would like."

"Why can't we try to be friends?" she asked. He gaped. "Hear me out. We might not end up the best of friends, and I know we're going to have to try to kill each other, but that's the spirits' deal. The spirits don't have to like each other, but I don't see why *we* can't be friends."

"That is… unprecedented," he said carefully.

"I suppose. In the end, we won't have any choice but to fight, but I don't see why we can't try to be friends before then. It's more pleasant than hating each other. If you're gonna be around me so much, I think we should at least be on friendly terms."

Connor gazed thoughtfully at her. She fiddled with strands of grass, braiding them as a slow blush crept further across her cheeks the longer he was silent.

"I guess," he finally said, unconsciously ruffling his hair. Amy smiled and he let out a breath. "Why would you ask such a thing?"

"I couldn't help myself. You're a royal pain and can be a jerk, but I'm happy to have a friend that understands all this spirit crap. None of my friends know about it."

"That's probably for the best," he agreed. "Do you have a lot of friends, then?"

"Are you going to get jealous if I do?" she teased, standing and brushing herself off.

"Why would I get jealous over you?" He stood as well, and she rolled her eyes.

"If you must know, I don't have a lot of friends. I have a few people I say hi to in school, but my best friends are Satomi and Adam, not counting my brother, Arty. What about you?"

"As I said, I don't really have any friends. Training to be the Sword doesn't leave much time for friendships."

"Or social skills." Now Connor rolled his eyes as she chuckled.

"I have amazing social skills. I just don't use them on you."

"That's not very nice."

"I am not very nice."

Amy stuck her tongue out at him. Connor barked out a laugh, looking surprised. "So, are you not going to be very nice to me?" Amy's face had become serious.

He paused and looked at her thoughtfully. He thought about it long enough that Amy had to look away. She'd begun to fidget with her shirt again by the time he responded. He walked up to her and put a hand under her chin, lifting her face like he had when they first met. They stared at each other without movement. "I think I will be nice to you," he said at last. "I wasn't raised to be nice, but perhaps I'll try with you." She fought back the heat rising across her cheeks. She jerked her head away and stepped back.

"I need to go." Her thoughts were jumbled, and she was growing tired of blushing.

"Would you like me to escort you to the park's entrance?"

"Why? So you can figure out where I live?" she replied lightly, a half-smile on her face.

"Please don't take this the wrong way, but I'm pretty sure the Sheath already knows where you live." She paled. "Don't worry, they won't do anything. They're only around to support the Sword."

"Reassuring." He shrugged at her comment. "But seriously, I need to get going. I've already stayed longer than I meant to, and I'm sure Arty's wondering where I am." She started to walk away, and Connor followed.

"How old is your brother?"

"Thirty-four."

"Quite the age difference."

"Yep, I was a miracle child. My parents shouldn't have been able to have a second kid and yet, here I am." She held her arms out wide and struck a pose. "Arty has raised me since I was four, so sometimes he's more dad-like."

"Is that when—"

"Yeah, that's when my parents died." She didn't question how he knew. They reached a fork in the path, and she turned away from him. "Good night, Connor."

"Good night, Amy."

She walked away briskly. *Can I trust him? Should I trust him? The Sword and the Sheath are dangerous but is Connor?* Her phone rang, jolting her back to reality.

"Where are you?" Arty asked as soon as she answered. "I've been waiting forever."

"I'm sorry, Arty," she said. "I got distracted and lost track of time. I'm almost there."

"Distracted doing what?"

Her mind raced. Should she tell the truth? "I ran into a friend from school."

"Anyone I know?"

"Nope."

"You can tell me about them later, hurry up."

Amy hung up. She wasn't sure what to make of Connor and her stomach knotted the more she thought about her fate. Sometimes, she got so scared that she almost couldn't breathe. *Does Connor ever get scared?* She doubted it, he was so brainwashed.

15
Connor

CONNOR SETTLED INTO HIS SEAT AS THE DOOR was closed behind him. He bowed his head once at his father.

"Father," he said politely.

"These trips out are a waste of time. You need to be at home, training for the glory of the Sword." His voice was cold, and his eyes were narrowed.

Connor's heart was in his throat, and he felt something he couldn't quite identify bubble up inside him as he thought about no longer seeing Amy at the park. He kept his face neutral as he replied. "I understand, Father, but the park is where I can see Am—the Shield girl alone. She's opening up to me. I think abandoning the park would mean abandoning the plan of gaining her confidence. I can't break her emotionally if we're not close."

His father went quiet for several tense minutes. Connor looked out the window, feigning disinterest as his heart thumped in his ears. He forcibly kept his knee from bouncing. Finally, Preston threw his head back and laughed. Connor almost flinched at the grating sound.

"I will have to confer with the other elders, but it sounds like you've done well. I retract my earlier command. You may continue to frequent the park as often as you need, it appears to be beneficial. But don't let your training slack, you need to be in perfect condition for the Sword."

"Yes, Father." Tension left Connor's muscles, and his breathing became easier.

16

Amy

HE SPIRIT BECAME INSISTENT ON INCREASED training, not being pleased with Amy's progress. And Amy was starting to get frustrated. The spirit had her doing body-weight exercises between working on energy blasts. The air was frigid, and her shoes were damp from the wet grass. She was simultaneously too hot and covered with goose bumps.

"Send a blast toward that tree," the spirit commanded, drawing her attention toward the one it wanted. The voice was apathetic, but Amy thought she caught a faint hint of irritation, which only increased her own.

Amy ground her teeth, her chest tightening as her cheeks burned. She wanted to scream. Out of nowhere, she remembered Connor's advice from the night before and gathered a glowing orb into her hand. Pulling her arm back, she launched the sphere at the tree, which promptly cracked. This was by far the best blast she had produced, and she was rather proud of it.

"*Where did you learn that?*" the spirit demanded.

"*I ran into Connor last night, and he suggested it. Aren't you always in my head?*" she asked in her mind.

"*I am not always awake. What do you mean you met with the Sword again?*"

Amy explained what happened. It was useless lying to something in her own mind. "He just sort of appears where I am. It's quite annoying but hanging out with him isn't too bad."

"*What do you mean you 'hung out' with the Sword of Darkness? He is a tool of destruction. He and the Sheath want to destroy life, and you are hanging out with him... for fun?!*" Wincing, Amy covered her ears as if that would protect her from the yelling within.

"He's a tool just like me," she tried to explain, wringing her hands. "We're both pawns for you spirits. It's nice to have a friend even if he's a tota—"

"*You think that that thing is your friend?!*"

Heat rushed through her body. "I do. The Sword certainly isn't, but Connor and I are. We're becoming friends, anyway."

There was another long pause. "*You... you senseless, naïve, stupid girl.*" The spirit's rage laced its tone. "*You think you can be friends with the vessel of darkness? Are you dense? He is probably trying to befriend you to weaken you for a better chance of killing you! Do you not understand that the fate of the universe rests on your shoulders? How did I end up with such a stupid host? This is unprecedented!*"

The heat rushing through Amy's veins turned into an inferno. Her mind raced as she thought of all that she'd been through since this parasite had infested her. All the lies. The fear. The loneliness. All these things boiled over, and she glowed a vibrant, red-tinged gold and floated into the air.

"Then maybe you should find a new host." Her mind grew eerily quiet as she focused on the center of her chest.

"Amy, what are you doing? Wait—"

"No, I'm done waiting. I'm done with your crap. And I am done with *you*. I'm doing my best. How *dare* you treat me this way. How *dare* you call me stupid. I think you need a time out." Grabbing as much power as she could control, she shoved the Shield's awareness as far into her mind as she could, imagining slamming and locking a steel door on it. The spirit didn't have time to get a word out before being silenced. Its presence receded in her mind, and she was truly alone in her own head for the first time in months.

She was stuck in the blazing glow of rage-fueled power for several more minutes, breathing deeply and shaking, struggling to get herself under control. It was all she could do to keep the energy from violently expanding outward and destroying everything in its path. Tears burned down her cheeks as her limbs shook.

"Amy?"

She opened blazing eyes to see Connor, his mouth gaping and eyes wide. He had his hands up in front of him. Her power blazed in reaction to the Sword's presence. "Amy, I sensed you losing control across the park. Please, take a deep breath and try to calm down." He was panting, his breath fogging the air around him as sweat trickled down the side of his face.

"Calm down?!" she shrieked, turning on him, the power blazing even brighter. Connor flinched and a gray energy swirled around him. His face softened to a neutral expression as his breathing evened. "We are being set up to *die,* and you want me to *calm down*?!"

"Well... yes." He floated to her level, his mouth drawn into a frown. "I understand this is scary. You haven't had the time to adjust that I have, but I've felt the same things and would assume the past hosts did as well."

"You felt this way?" The power swirling around her slowed and her voice wavered.

"Yes and blowing up this park will *not* make you feel any better."

Amy closed her eyes, and the energy began to recede into her body, the red tinge faded, and she lowered to the ground. She stood on the browning grass for several minutes before the glow around her went out completely, and she collapsed, breathing hard but sitting up. Connor hesitantly dropped and withdrew his power, going to kneel within a few feet of her.

She focused on the ground, fighting to keep from crying more or passing out. Connor placed his hand on her shoulder and she flinched as she looked up at him. He jerked his hand back and blushed.

"I'm sorry, you startled me." She reached out to him, then brought her hand back, unsure of what she meant to do. "Thanks for helping me."

"Uh, no problem."

She sank forward onto the ground and rested her head on her arm. "Amy!" he exclaimed, shaking her shoulder.

"Stop that," she mumbled. He let out a breath and removed his hand. "You should be happy. Look how easy I am to kill. You may very well be the first Sword to break the Shield." Her voice was bitter as she turned her face into the grass. She curled into herself and held her knees to her chest while her whole body heaved.

"I don't really want you to die," he admitted. She moved her head to be able to look slightly up at him, one eyebrow raised.

"I have to die for you to win."

"And I must die for you to win." Their usual awkward silence returned. Unable to bear it, Amy struggled to sit up but had to clutch her head when she finally got into a seated position. Pressure from the center of her brain felt like it was exploding outward. "I remember the headaches that came when I first got my powers. They were the worst."

"I'll say," she said, hunching over. "When do they stop?"

"To be honest, they come back if you overdo things, but they become rarer as you progress."

"It has been a while." She shook her head and looked up at him. "The spirit usually helps me get rid of them, but I think I've chased her off."

"My teachers have that skill as well. The Sword isn't... particularly interested in my pain."

"Teachers? And they have powers?" She winced. It made sense that a malevolent spirit of darkness wouldn't show much compassion, even to its host.

"Kind of? They can tap into the Sword's energies a little

bit, and some of the elders can even communicate with it a bit. Being in an ancient organization that's had time to study my spirit has to have some perks," he said with a half-smile. She smiled fully in return as the headache cleared. Connor stood and held a hand out to her. She took it and each host managed to keep their spirit's power from reacting.

"Ha! We managed to touch without blowing ourselves up." She squeezed his hand, and Connor smiled fully, lighting up his face. Her eyes went wide. "You should do that more often," she blurted, her face coloring immediately as she cast her eyes downward.

"Pardon me, but do what?"

"Smile. You look nicer when you smile. It almost hides that you can be a jerk."

Connor barked out a laugh. He still had her hand, and she wasn't quite sure what to do about it. He seemed to realize at the same time because he jerked his hand back and ran it through his hair. *So much for the smooth and classy act.*

"I should go before Arty gets worried. I'm not making much progress in my training anyway." She felt some color leave her cheeks. "Probably shouldn't have said that, huh?"

"You should stop blabbing things." He gave her another half-smile.

"Probably. I've really gotta go," Amy said, checking the time on her phone. "Wanna sit with me at lunch tomorrow?" He looked at her, clearly surprised.

"Are you sure?"

"Yeah, I think Satomi'll like you. Are you okay not sitting with your friends?"

He looked thoughtful for a moment. "Oh, you mean Peter and Quinton?"

"Is that who you normally sit with?"

"Yes, I think they would appreciate a break from me," he said. "They only sit with me because they have to and as you know, I'm not nice. I would like to sit with you and Satomi."

"It's a date." She could have kicked herself for using that phrase.

"May I walk you to the park entrance?" he asked. "It's starting to get dark."

"I can defend myself against nearly any creep, but sure, I wouldn't mind." They headed down the nearest path, careful to stay a couple of feet apart. Amy wasn't quite sure what to say and neither spoke as they walked. They moved in an amicably awkward silence down the winding path until they reached the park entrance closest to her apartment. They paused there.

The sun was setting, which meant the park was closing soon. "Thanks for the gentlemanly escort," Amy said teasingly. "Should I like, curtsy or something?"

He laughed and, with a smirk, gave her a flawless, sweeping bow. "'Twas a pleasure, my lady."

She laughed. "Knock it off! Have a good night, see you at lunch tomorrow."

"Good night."

17

Amy

As lunch approached, Amy wasn't sure she'd be able to eat around the knot forming in her stomach. Last night, she hadn't thought about the implications of sitting with Connor in front of everyone, but now it was too late to cancel, and she didn't have his phone number anyway. The school wasn't very big, so any and all gossip was precious. Amy didn't want to be the newest topic of gossip by hanging out with a handsome upperclassman who was also relatively newer to town. At the thought of the stares, a cold sweat coated her forehead.

As her mind wandered off to peruse all the ways that this could go horribly wrong, the lunch bell rang, and Amy almost leapt out of her seat. An entire field's worth of butterflies had suddenly been let loose in her stomach. She met Satomi in the hallway.

"You okay?" Satomi asked after one glance at Amy, who shrugged.

"Yeah, I'll go get the table while you buy lunch." Amy gestured to the cafeteria with her lunch bag.

Satomi eyed her. "You seem nervous."

"Nope, not at all," she squeaked. "I'll see you at the table." She veered away from Satomi and into the cafeteria. She was too flustered to try to think strategically about a location that would garner the least amount of attention.

"We're talking about this when I get there!" Satomi shouted at her retreating back before hurrying to the growing line.

Amy sat at an empty table off to the side and sighed in relief. She slumped in the cold, hard chair and closed her eyes.

"Good afternoon, Amy," Connor said from behind her.

"AH!" Amy almost fell out of her chair. Connor's eyebrows shot up.

"You are jumpy. Are you nervous for our lunch date?" He winked. Amy scowled at him and turned back to the table.

"This isn't a date," she muttered. "And don't try to use that fake charm on me. Friends sit together and we're becoming friends." He chuckled and sat beside her, getting his lunch out of his backpack. "I thought a rich boy like you would buy lunch," Amy blurted. She clapped her hands over her mouth, feeling her cheeks burn hotter. "I'm so sorry. I didn't mean to say that out loud." She would never get control over her stupid mouth when she was nervous.

Connor threw back his head and laughed loudly. "Please, don't apologize," he said, still chuckling. "It's hard to get the proper nutrients from school food, so I bring my lunch. If it makes you feel any better, a servant usually prepares it for me." Amy removed her hands from her burning face.

"Huh, that makes sense. I don't like to waste money, so I bring my own. Besides, the vegetarian food here is pretty much only salad."

"I don't know your brother, but I don't imagine he would think of feeding his sister as wasting money." He looked at her thoughtfully, unwrapping his gourmet meal.

"Perhaps," she conceded while unpacking her lunch but not making eye contact. "But you can't deny that cafeteria food is overpriced."

"Amy!"

Amy considered acting like she hadn't heard Satomi. Satomi slammed her tray down and smacked Amy's arm. Connor raised his eyebrows.

"Ow, Satomi! What the heck?!" Amy glared up at her best friend, rubbing her sore arm. "What was that for?"

"Is *he* what you were being so weird about?!" she asked, waving a wild hand at Connor, her bright green sleeves a blur. *Darn it, Satomi, you loudmouth.*

"Stop yelling. I wasn't being weird," Amy snapped.

"Yes, you were. Hi, Connor," Satomi said, switching to a more pleasant tone and taking her seat. "Welcome to the loser table." Amy slammed her head onto the hard surface of the table and left it there.

"Thank you, Satomi," he responded. "It's my pleasure to be here. Amy invited me to join the two of you for lunch last night at the park. I hope you don't mind."

"Oh? Last night at the park, huh?" Satomi asked teasingly, elbowing Amy.

"Please kill me," Amy groaned.

"We ran into each other again, and since we keep seeing each other so often, Amy invited me to make the friendship official."

"Really?" Satomi said, sounding like Christmas had come early.

Amy sat up and glared at her. "Satomi, leave it," she said. "I don't know why you have to assume I'm dating every guy that talks to me." Connor choked on his salad, and Satomi snorted.

"Well, you only have two guy friends now, so that's not much of a sample size."

"Oh for—just eat your food," Amy said, viciously biting into her sandwich. "How has your day been so far, Connor?" she asked once she had finished the bite, ignoring Satomi who was still giggling.

His face was fairly neutral, but he had a slightly puzzled look in his eyes. "My day has been going well, thank you for asking. Yours?"

"Oh, same old."

"Is Adam your other guy friend?" he asked.

Satomi half choked on her food.

"Yes. Satomi has this stupid idea that he likes me, but we're just friends." He stared at her, then raised an eyebrow with an expression that clearly said he thought the same.

"He's totally into you," Satomi snarked through a mouth full of french fries. Amy was used to her lack of manners, but Connor grimaced as he watched bits of potatoes fly from her mouth.

"I think you want us to get together to give you cute niblings." Amy chuckled. Satomi choked on her food again. "You wouldn't choke so much if you ate like a civilized human."

Satomi guffawed, more potatoes flying out. "Don't be ridiculous," she spluttered. "I don't see his appeal." Amy smacked her arm.

"Be nice, he's my *friend*."

Satomi wiped her face with a napkin. "So, Connor, what do you like to do for fun?" Amy was grateful for the subject change.

He paused. "I do martial arts and some extracurricular studying, like languages. I'm finishing Mandarin currently."

"That's cool. My parents have me study Japanese outside of school too," Satomi replied. Amy picked at her food, unwillingly curious about what Connor would say next. "Do you have hobbies? I sculpt and like anime, and Amy paints."

"You paint?" he asked Amy, deflecting the question.

She nodded, then swallowed more of the sandwich. "I do. I'm okay at it, but I like to walk around the park to get inspiration, which is why you keep seeing me there." He nodded, acknowledging the partial lie.

Adam plopped into a seat at their table, smiling at Amy before glaring slightly at Connor.

"Hey, Ames, this guy bothering you again?" Adam asked. Amy caught Connor's frown from the corner of her eye, as she turned a placating smile on Adam.

"Hey Adam, I invited Connor to sit with us. We see each other at the park so much that we've become friends." Connor raised an eyebrow at her, and she grinned, placing a hand on his forearm. Tension and power radiated off him, though she couldn't tell why. Touch might not be his thing she realized belatedly as she quickly removed her hand.

Adam's eyes lingered on where Amy's hand had rested. He perked up. "Think you'll be able to come to my wrestling meet tomorrow?"

"Where's it at?"

"Barrington."

Amy couldn't suppress a frown. "I'm sorry. Arty's working on a big project at work right now, so I won't be able to."

"You need to get on him to get you a car. You should have gotten one at your sweet sixteen like I did."

Amy rubbed her arm, looking down, heat building in her chest.

"Fancy things aren't everything," she replied with a shake of her hair. "I don't really need a car. It's not a big deal, I like walking and taking the bus."

"I'd die without a car."

Amy rolled her eyes at him. "Perhaps you're spoiled."

"Ain't nothing wrong with that," Adam said with a hearty chuckle. Amy resisted the urge to frown. Not everyone had rich parents. Or parents, for that matter. "I gotta go and catch up with the guys. I'll see you around, okay?"

"See ya," Amy said somewhat icily. Adam looked uncomfortable but left anyway.

"What a jerk," Satomi said, then she looked apologetically at Amy. "I'm sorry. I know you're friends, but he gets on my nerves."

"Mine too, sometimes. But he can't help it, it's how he grew up. He's kind under all that bravado."

"If you say so," Satomi said, standing up with her tray. She threw away her trash and returned her tray while Amy and Connor packed up. "So, how'd you like sitting at the loser table?" she asked Connor when she returned.

"I wouldn't call either of you losers," he replied with a slight smile. "I wouldn't mind sitting here again."

"Go for it. You're an okay dude," Satomi declared. Amy beamed, happy to see at least two of her friends getting along. The bell rang.

"To art!" Satomi yelled, pointing toward their classroom as she charged forward. People jumped out of her way as she barreled through. Amy covered her mouth and laughed. Nothing could get between Satomi and art.

"How did you two become friends?" Connor asked.

"We've been friends forever," Amy said dismissively. "We met in kindergarten. She pushed a mean boy that was teasing me and then we played hide and seek. We've been best friends, practically sisters, ever since." A warm glow spread through her as she thought about that day. "We both love art, so that's what we bond over."

"She seems like a very interesting person. I would like to see some of your work sometime." Amy eyed him, but he seemed genuinely interested.

"Sure," she said. "But you can't laugh, okay?"

"Scout's honor," he replied, mock saluting her with a grin.

"Like you were a scout," she said with a laugh, shoving him playfully. He smiled as he caught himself.

18

Amy

Satomi accosted Amy as soon as she entered the art room, glomming onto her arm, and throwing her off balance.

"Oh Ames, he's *gorgeous*," she said, pulling Amy toward their table. Amy rolled her eyes as she stumbled along after her, worried that her arm might come out of its socket.

"How have you already gotten clay on your sweater?" Amy asked, ignoring Satomi's admiration of Connor.

"Don't try to distract me." Satomi flopped onto her stool at their station and looked over her sculpture, touching it up here and there.

"I'm not distracting from anything, there's nothing to talk about," she said, shooting a fierce glare at her best friend. "Drop it."

Satomi sighed. "You're no fun."

"You're too *much* fun." Amy paused, and they both laughed.

—

ER POWER REACTED TO CONNOR'S PRESENCE before she saw him, and she spun to see him coming toward her in the bus bay. She broke into a smile, reflexively shoving the energy down like a disobedient dog. Silencing it was easy, ignoring its silent reactions was not.

"Don't you fancy rich boys take cars home?" she teased. He chuckled.

"We do. I wanted to come see when I can view some of your art."

"I thought you were being polite." Amy's stomach fluttered with more than her power's reaction.

"No, I've decided not to be polite with you."

"So, I get to see the *real* Connor?"

"Sure," he replied. She looked at him for a moment.

"Come home with me," she said.

Connor's eyes looked like they were about to bug out of his head. "Pardon?" he choked out.

"Come home with me. My bus will be here any minute, board it and come with me. My driver never pays attention. I'll show you my art and then we can go to the park before Arty comes home." She grinned widely. Arty would kill her if he knew she brought a boy home, even if it was just to show him some art.

A bus with the number five on it pulled up, and she moved toward it, stopping to turn around.

"You coming?" she asked.

Connor boarded the bus with her in an obvious daze. She led him to one of the seats in front and she scooted in. He scooted in jerkily after her. Looking around, he patted the vinyl seat.

"Where are the seat belts?" he asked.

"Seriously?" she replied. "Have you never ridden a bus?"

He flushed. "Well, no."

"Oh. School buses and public buses don't have seat belts. They're so big and high up that we're safe. On public buses, if it's too crowded, you stand in the aisles and hold on to poles or handles above your head." She tried not to sound patronizing while she explained, but it was hard.

"I have seen people standing on buses when I've driven past them."

"Silly rich boy." She nudged him with her elbow. "What's it like to be rich?"

He thought for a moment, staring off into space. Amy used this time to examine him. She had managed not to look too closely at him before now and took this time to examine him. He had sharp features and a defined jaw. His hair was a deep shade of brown with natural highlights, his skin slightly tanned and flawless. Her hand itched with the urge to sketch him.

She blushed furiously and jerked her head toward the window. Connor glanced at her.

"What?" he asked, cocking his head to the side.

"Nothing," she said. "So, what's it like?" She couldn't look him in the eye.

"I don't know," he replied with a shrug. "I've never been anything else. What is it like not being rich?"

"Normal?" Amy responded, finally working up the nerve to look at him again. "We're not poor, and I have a good life, but it would be nice to have some fancy things."

"Like a car?" he asked.

She went scarlet. "Like a car."

"Tell me, will you not ask your brother for anything because he doesn't have a lot of money or because you feel indebted to him?" She looked at him sharply.

"Wha—what?" she stammered.

"It's pretty obvious you don't like asking for things."

"You got all that from meeting me a handful of times?" He nodded.

"You're not wrong. Arty was really young when he took me in. He was only twenty-two at the time, but he took me in and finished college while caring for me. He gave up a lot to make sure we stayed together."

"I had no idea," he murmured.

"I'm sorry, I'm used to everyone just knowing, small towns being what they are." She looked out the window. "My stop is next, grab your bag."

The bus came to a halt, and Amy followed Connor off the bus with butterflies winging wildly in her abdomen.

He looked around. "Where do you live?"

"Over there," she said, pointing at a beige building a few blocks away. "Come on," she said, leading him to a cross-walk, across the street, and to her home. Connor looked bewildered. She noticed this and raised an eyebrow at him. "Have you never been inside an apartment before?" He mutely shook his head. She stopped outside of her unit and unlocked the door.

"Welcome to my humble abode!" she declared as she dropped her bag by the entryway.

"You have a lovely home," he said automatically. She rolled her eyes and elbowed him.

"Shove off, McMansion."

"What? I was being serious."

"Come on, I'll give you the grand tour." She felt her heart rate kick up as she realized that he'd be the first boy to ever see her room. Adam had never come over to her place at all.

She led Connor down the hall, pointing out the living room and the bathroom before opening her bedroom door, and she thanked her lucky stars that she had cleaned it. She gestured around her. "Behold, my art gallery. Remember, you promised not to laugh. All the original paintings on the walls were done by yours truly."

Connor walked in tentatively, looking overwhelmed by the amount of art and posters. The sky blue of her walls was barely visible. He paused, examining an unframed oil painting of the entrance to Whittaker Hills Park, staring at the painting for several seconds. "This is beautiful," he breathed, turning to look at her with bright eyes. It was the most animated Amy had ever seen him.

She looked over his shoulder. "Oh, that one? I did that one for class last year. Would you like it? I need to clear wall space." He looked incredulous.

"Are you serious?" He was so earnest and shocked that she couldn't help the flush that spread along her cheeks.

"Yeah, it's nothing special," she said, looking at the ground for a moment.

"Nothing special? Amy, this work is incredible." She couldn't help smiling shyly. Connor ran a hand through his hair, flushing slightly.

"If you like it so much, you can have it. It can put all your fancy, shmancy art to shame," she joked. She took it off the wall and handed it to him.

"And it shall," he said, taking the painting reverently from her. He looked around at the others. She had painted multiple landscape scenes of the park, as landscapes were her specialty. He looked at each one carefully, his expression awed.

"You're very talented," he said. She rummaged in her bag for a wrapped canvas.

"You inspired this one," she said. "I was mad at you when we first met and, well, it's abstract. I finally remembered to take it home." She handed the package to him, and he carefully unwrapped it. Inside was a small painting of a pitch-black circle surrounded by shimmering gold in a sea of flames. You could almost feel the despair coming off of it.

"I'm sorry this happened to you," he said at last. His forehead creased as he frowned.

"That what happened to me?" Amy cocked her head to the side, confused.

"This!" he exclaimed, gesturing violently at the painting. "The Shield. The Sword. The Sheath. All of it. I wish anyone else was the Shield. You don't deserve this." He ran a hand through his hair again as he paced, causing it to stick up at weird angles this time.

Amy's gaze turned serious. "Connor, you don't deserve this either. Neither of us asked for it, but here we are. Besides, if we weren't chosen, we never would have met, and we never would have become friends. That's something, isn't it?"

"Amy, do you not know how this ends for the hosts every time the spirits meet?" His eyes shined with raw emotion, his normal mask ripped away.

"I know there's a battle and one of us will likely die—" His eyes flashed. "Is there more?"

"Let's go to the park," he said abruptly. He took off his backpack and carefully put the painting of the park inside, moving things away from it.

"Connor, what's wrong?" Amy asked, grabbing a coat.

"Let's talk at the park, okay?" he said as he led her out of the apartment. His urgency propelled her onwards.

"What's wrong?" Amy repeated, jogging to keep up.

"I said we'll talk at the park."

"But—"

"Park."

They walked silently the rest of the way to the nearest entrance of the park and were soon walking amongst the many trails, making their way to the secluded area where Amy usually trained. Her stomach was in knots and her mind kept flashing to different possibilities.

When they finally stopped, Connor spoke. "Let us meditate."

Amy stomped a foot and crossed her arms. "Not before you tell me what's going on. I can't meditate right now, so tell me what's wrong."

He sank to the ground and crossed his long legs. "Please sit."

She sat across from him, also crossing her legs. "Spill. Why are you being weird, and why are we here?" She suppressed a frustrated sigh when he didn't answer right away and began to fiddle with the grass, forcing herself to give him time to think.

"Amy," he began with a slight look of apprehension. "I need you to remain calm and in control, okay? We're out here in case you cannot do that." She met his eyes. "When the final battle happens, it is very, *very* likely that neither of us will survive." She stared at him with wide eyes as coldness settled in her chest.

"During every battle thus far, the Shield has killed the Sword's vessel. The Sword has come close a few times, but the Shield has been stronger each time. Apparently, what was left out of your education," Connor started to sound faintly angry, "is that you will die too. Once the battle is over, the Shield, if it wins, will be too weak to keep possessing you. It will leave your battered body behind and, if you don't die from your wounds, you'll die when the spirit leaves. We don't know what will happen to me if the Sword wins since it never has before, but I imagine my fate would be similar after the Sword used me to destroy everything.

"We've had these spirits intertwined with our souls since the day we were conceived. No vessel has ever survived without one of the spirits. We will both die in the final battle, regardless of who wins. The next hosts don't need to be our direct descendants, so we will not be needed anymore after that point. There's always a distant cousin somewhere."

Numbness spread through Amy's body. Swaying, she caught herself with a hand on the ground. She stared at the grass with vacant eyes. Her thoughts were racing so fast that she couldn't decipher them. Pain radiated out from her chest.

After what felt like an eternity, she looked up as realization dawned on her. Connor blanched slightly at her face. "You've known this all along?" she asked, tears filling her eyes as her voice quavered.

"Yes, I've known since childhood."

"That we were born to die?"

"We were."

She was silent again. "You've known your whole life that you were born to be sacrificed?"

"I did," Connor said it so matter-of-factly that Amy felt her heart break for him. She had to resist the urge to reach out and hug him, she felt so wretched.

"I'm so sorry," she choked out, tears almost brimming over. "I am so, *so* sorry, Connor. How horrible it must've been to be told your whole life that your only purpose was to die." Amy felt the tears start to burn her eyes, so she shut them tightly, unsuccessfully trying to keep them from spilling over. They fell anyway. She scrubbed at her face with the heels of her hands.

Connor's face went pale, and he frowned. He sat upright and shook himself like a wet dog, then laughed. "You are dying, and you are crying because of me?"

She sniffed, looking at him while wiping her eyes. "You're dying too. I mean, I don't wanna die, and I'm scared, but at least I got to live without knowing I was just a sacrifice for a while." She scrubbed at her tearstained face, her cheeks already feeling raw.

As she watched Connor through her tears, his pale face transformed from shock to sadness. Without warning, his eyes narrowed, and his cheeks flushed red as black and gray energy burst from him, swirling shapelessly around his body.

Amy yelped and shot back, immediately glowing golden. He recalled his power, shaking. "I apologize," he said, looking at the ground.

"And you thought I'd be the one to lose control," she replied with a weak chuckle, more tears spilling down her face.

"I thought you would react a bit more like a normal person," he said, rolling his eyes. His mask was starting to come back.

Shrugging, she looked down. "At first, I was afraid, but then I realized it meant you had known your whole life, and it broke my heart, and I couldn't help myself."

Connor stared at her. "You need to stop," he said.

"Stop what?"

"Stop caring!" he snapped, his face flushing again. "You need to stop, Amy. You need to think about *you* more. You need to put yourself first. Look at you. You're alone with your biggest enemy in the middle of nowhere. You silly girl." His eyes burned into hers.

She smiled sadly, shrugging off the name he hurled at her. "If I don't care about you, who will?"

Without warning, Connor crumpled forward onto his knees, his face in his hands. Amy was shocked when she heard a small sob escape him.

She scooted beside him and rubbed his back. She allowed the tears to run down her face as she let him sob in silence. After some time, he quieted. Amy wasn't sure what to say, so she said nothing. Connor took out his phone. He groaned and set it face down on the ground, putting his head back into his hands.

"What is it?" Amy asked.

"My father called. I didn't tell anyone I wasn't coming home."

"Will you be in trouble?"

"I am too old and too powerful to be thrashed, so not entirely, no." Amy gasped.

"They hit you?"

Connor looked at her. "Yes, that's how children are taught." He caught Amy's look of horror and gave her a half smile. "I, uh, am starting to think that might have been a Sheath thing." She nodded mutely.

"Do you have to go home?"

"I do."

"I'm surprised Arty hasn't blown up my phone. He's used to me going to the park a lot though."

"What now?"

Amy thought for a moment. "Huh, I guess we really are friends now. I don't know that I've ever had such a jerk for a friend before, but I can deal with it," she said at last, teasingly. Connor looked at her before laughing.

"That's not what I was talking about, but sure, let's be 'besties,' as you would say."

Amy beamed at him before standing and brushing off her pants. She held out her hand reflexively to help him up. He looked at her with a half-raised eyebrow and smirk.

"I get it, you're taller than me. Now get up." Connor grabbed her hand and allowed her to help him stand. Or to pretend like she was helping, anyway.

"How are you getting home?" Amy asked as they walked out to the park entrance.

"I'll probably call for a car, though I would like to escort you the rest of the way to your home. It's not dark yet, but it's only proper."

"Connor, before I got these powers and met you, I walked alone. These streets and this park are as much my home as my apartment. I'm not scared of them, and I can handle myself."

"I didn't think you couldn't, but it's polite to escort a lady home." Amy rolled her eyes so hard that she thought she might pull something.

"Take your stereotypes and shove 'em," she responded flatly. "I'm walking home alone."

He sighed. "As you wish. Will I see you at lunch tomorrow?"

"Of course, you're one of us now," she said with a wink. "As Satomi would say, welcome to the loser table."

"You're not a loser, Amy," Connor said, his face turning serious.

She laughed. "In high school terms, Satomi and I are losers, but we're okay with it. Being popular and charming like you seems like an awful lot of work." It was Connor's turn to roll his eyes, and she giggled. "Good night, bestie. I'll see you tomorrow."

"Good night, Amy," he said with a wave as she quickly walked off toward her apartment.

19

Connor

CONNOR SIGHED AS HE TOOK OUT HIS PHONE to call Roland—he would have to go home and face the music sooner or later. Ignoring the knot forming in his stomach, he made the call.

Soon, a black SUV pulled up, and his face had transformed back into a look of cold indifference. Roland got out, quickly maneuvering around the vehicle toward Connor, who waited with a look of slight impatience that he had learned from his father.

"Mr. Connor," Roland said deferentially with a nod as he opened the door. Connor ignored him as he climbed into the seat and buckled himself in. They left the park and drove back to the manor in silence. He kept the look of indifference on his face, but inside, his stomach churned, and his heart rate accelerated.

Once his powers manifested, his father had switched tactics and expected Connor to take charge and make decisions regarding Sheath business on his own—with oversight of course. After a lifetime of being beaten and torn down, it was not an easy transition.

The car pulled into Whittaker Estates and drove up Connor's long driveway. The perfectly manicured landscapes looked hideous to him now that he had seen the real beauty of the park through Amy's eyes. She'd captured the essence of the more natural looking park perfectly in her painting, drawing his awareness to it.

Roland pulled up in front of the house and then hurried to open Connor's door. Connor ignored the older man again as the front doors opened and Bertram stepped out.

"Good evening, Mr. Connor," he said pleasantly.

"Good evening, Bertram."

"Your father is waiting for you in the parlor," Bertram continued. "He would like an explanation regarding your absence."

"Of course he would. I shall go and see him immediately."

"Very good, Mr. Connor. Please, bear your father's temper in mind when you speak to him."

"Of course."

He found his father lounging in a high-backed chair, sipping tea. "Father," Connor said, nodding his head. His father looked up at him with narrowed eyes but didn't speak. Connor fought the urge to roll his own eyes. He still had homework to do and didn't have time for this. He stared right back, unflinching.

At last, Preston set his teacup down. "You did not come home," he stated.

"I did not." If his father wanted answers, let him ask the questions. Preston stared at him with piercing green eyes the same shade as his own. Just yesterday, Connor would have broken eye contact first, but today, his strength was bolstered by his anger, and he didn't have energy for his father's games. After several moments of intense eye contact, his father grinned. The smile looked cruel rather than pleased.

"It's good to see you're developing a backbone," he said approvingly, taking another sip of tea. The tea was strong, and the scent tickled Connor's nose. "Where were you?"

"I was with the Shield girl. The Sheath's orders were to get closer to her and I have."

"Elaborate."

Connor paused a moment, thinking of what to say. "She believes that I'm her friend and asked me to accompany her to the park after school. I didn't have time to contact any Sheath members before leaving. As the Sword, I made the decision to go with her. Nothing of importance happened. The Shield girl continues to believe me her friend."

"Excellent. Go get dinner and then attend to your studies."

"Of course, Father." Without a backward glance, Connor left the room and went to find Bertram, who was cooking in the kitchen. From the smell of it, Bertram was cooking Connor's favorite dinner—spaghetti with meatballs. He suppressed a smile.

"Hello, Bertram," Connor said. "I hope that spaghetti is for me."

Bertram beamed at Connor with an almost fatherly look on his face. "Of course, Connor. I thought you might need some fortification after meeting with your father." The servitude façade always dropped when they were alone.

"It went alright," Connor said, leaning against the counter to watch Bertram work.

"Really?" Bertram asked.

"Yeah," Connor said without elaborating before sitting at one of the servant tables. The Callaghans never ate with servants, but Connor sometimes broke the rules to be with Bertram.

Bertram bustled around the kitchen and soon placed a plate of whole wheat spaghetti and lean meatballs in front of Connor with a big, leafy green salad. "I wanted to give you some comfort food, but I know how you are about your nutrition."

Connor blushed. "You didn't have to go out of your way like that."

"It wasn't any trouble," Bertram said with a dismissive wave of his hand. "Just eat."

Connor ate and savored every bite. Bertram might not have been the family's chef, but he had always been the best chef in the world in Connor's eyes. Connor took a moment to sit back in contentment. "Thank you very much, Bertram," Connor said with a small smile. Bertram walked by and messed up his hair affectionately. Connor swatted at him irritably, rearranging his hair as Bertram laughed.

"You're very welcome. Now go do your homework."

Connor rolled his eyes but smiled. "Whatever. Good night, Bertram."

"Good night, Connor."

Connor made it to his room and looked around, noticing how plain it looked in comparison to Amy's. He had a four-poster bed in the center, and the walls were mostly bare, aside from a few tasteful paintings in gilded frames. He took down the smallest one and took a closer look at it. It was a castle on a distant hill, an ancient Sheath holding. It looked to be about the same size as Amy's landscape painting.

He set the painting down and went to his bookbag, carefully removing Amy's painting of the park entrance. He went back to the castle painting and removed it from its frame, discarding it carelessly to the side. He placed Amy's painting in the golden frame almost reverently and put it back on the wall. Standing back, he admired his handiwork. In his mind, her art deserved such a frame.

He then removed the second of Amy's paintings from his bag and regarded it. He hadn't meant to take it, but there it was. He'd have to return it at some point, he supposed. It made his chest burn to look at, but he also didn't want to get rid of it.

He placed it in a drawer with the castle painting. No one came into his room other than to clean, so he was confident no one would notice the paintings. If they did, they wouldn't care. He sat down at his desk, took out the books for his advanced classes, and started his homework. His earlier dalliance with Amy meant he would be up later, but it was worth it.

20

Amy

A FEW WEEKS LATER, AMY'S ALARM WENT OFF much too early for a Saturday, jarring her awake. She sat up woozily, rubbing her eyes and yawning loudly. The bed was perfectly warm, and she desperately wanted to curl back under her blanket. Quick footsteps came down the hall and her door banged open, startling her. Arty, dressed in all his favorite lime green running gear, barged in.

"I heard your alarm!" he exclaimed. "Are you still sure you want to come?" Amy could feel the energy buzzing off him and she half-hated it because it was too early in the morning.

Amy stretched, yawning. "Of course! You've been dreaming of this for like, ever. There's no way I'm going to miss your big race." She stood, stretched again, and felt her back crack nicely. "Now go away so I can get dressed."

"I'll get your breakfast ready." Arty dashed out of the room. She groaned as she walked to her dresser. There wasn't time for a shower. She put on the special shirt she'd made with Satomi and smiled before covering it up with a navy zipped-up jacket. She put her hair into a ponytail with a bright blue scrunchie, donned her favorite jeans and sneakers, then walked out to the kitchen.

Arty set out a bowl of her favorite cereal, some fruit, and oat milk. He almost looked like he was doing the potty dance waiting for her. She laughed.

"Relax, we have plenty of time," she said, pouring her milk into the cereal bowl.

"I've been training for this half-marathon for *months*, Ames. I've been dreaming for even *longer* about qualifying for the marathon if I do well. I can't relax. We absolutely can*not* be late, and we still have to get Satomi." He fidgeted more, checking that his race bib was secure. As Amy chewed her first bite, he went over and double-checked everything in his backpack.

"I know how important this is, but you need to relax. Here, I'll eat faster." She chewed with overdone zeal, swallowed, and took in another huge mouthful.

"Don't choke," he half admonished with a chuckle. "Did you text Satomi?"

"No. I'll do it now." She took out her phone and shot Satomi a quick message asking if she was awake. Satomi replied with a deluge of emojis, causing Amy to smile with her overly full mouth. She swallowed, grimacing as the too big bite slowly went down. "She's up."

"Good."

Amy finished eating and Arty did her dishes while she

grabbed her navy mini backpack. He then all but dragged her from the apartment to Satomi's house, the car full of Arty's nervous excitement.

Satomi lived in the suburbs of Whittaker in a beige, two-story home. The yard, as always, was perfectly manicured. Amy texted Satomi as they pulled up, and she almost immediately burst out of the front door carrying a garbage bag that clearly held something large and flat. Amy could hear her yelling goodbye to her parents before she dashed out. She opened the door to the backseat where Amy was waiting for her, and shoved the bag at Amy before getting buckled in.

"All set to go, Captain Arty!" she cooed. Turning to Amy, she said, "I packed snacks!"

"Oh, thank God. I completely forgot, and I don't want any of Arty's weird gel things."

"I wouldn't share them with you anyway," he snarked back. "I need those for fuel for this running machine!" He gestured down at his long, thin frame.

Amy rolled her eyes. "Train for a few months and suddenly you think you're Hermes." Arty laughed. "You're gonna do great."

Satomi cheered. "We'll be rooting for you at the finish line!"

They drove for forty-five minutes to Barrington, singing along to the radio. They pulled into a parking garage near the starting line, and Arty checked and double-checked his race bib and backpack as they got out of the car. The buzz of the crowd was almost overwhelming.

"Relax, it'll be fine because—" Amy began and then she and Satomi dramatically unzipped their jackets to reveal matching shirts that they had made. They were neon-green with puffy paint and glitter galore. Each shirt read, "ARTY IS THE BEST!" in big bubble letters. Satomi took the signs out of the bag and handed one to Amy. The signs read "GO ARTY!" and "YOU CAN DO IT ARTY!" and were similarly decorated. Arty covered his face with both hands.

"Girls, that's so sweet of you," he said, hugging them both. "I already feel more motivated. I can finish this whole thing, no problem!" He looked at his watch. "I have to go check in and then line up. You two need to stay close to the finish line so we won't get separated when I'm done. Do you both have your phones?" Amy was torn between rolling her eyes and smiling at his immediate switch into dad mode.

"How else would we text people or post things?" Satomi asked, holding hers up.

Arty laughed. "I suppose you wouldn't leave home without them," he conceded. "Stick together as much as possible, okay?"

"Okay," they chorused.

"Let's take a few pictures before you head off," Amy said, taking her phone out and handing it to Satomi. Arty put up with photos for about three minutes before saying he really needed to get going and bolting for the check-in desk.

"Should we try to get seats on the curb?" Amy asked as she watched him get in line. There was a veritable sea of bodies near the starting line.

"What's his normal time?"

"Somewhere between an hour and a half and two hours, I can't remember."

"I am not sitting on a curb for that long, I think moving around would be better."

Satomi grabbed Amy's hand and started to drag her off, but Amy froze, sensing him before she saw him. Her eyes scanned the crowd and stopped when they met a pair of emerald eyes that widened when they locked on hers. Connor was standing in the crowd with the boys from the Sheath nearby. They followed his gaze, and their mouths popped open when they saw Amy.

"Connor?" she gasped. Satomi stopped and turned around. Connor was coming through the crowd toward them, leaving Peter and Quinton behind. He waved and she immediately changed direction to greet him.

"Connor! What are you doing here?" Satomi squealed, clapping her hands and bouncing up and down. "Are you here to cheer on Arty too?"

"Um, no... I didn't realize he was competing," he said, gesturing to his race bib.

"You're running the race?" Amy asked, eyeing him suspiciously.

"Yes." He raised an eyebrow.

"And you're not doing anything... untoward?" He gaped at her for a moment before laughing a deep, full laugh. Amy could see Peter and Quinton flinch as they drew closer, though they didn't fully approach.

Satomi looked confused, her head tilted to one side. "Untoward?" she repeated, looking at Amy, who grimaced.

Connor straightened but was still laughing. "No, I am not doing anything *untoward*. I'm running a fair race." Amy narrowed her eyes more, and he rolled his in return. "I promise you, Amy, I'll be running a perfectly *normal* race. Having accomplishments looks good for college admissions."

"Good," she said, smiling. "Though I am sorry we didn't bring any signs or make shirts for you. I bet I have markers in my bag somewhere, though." She looked away to begin rummaging around in her backpack.

"Why do I feel like I missed something?" Satomi asked, still looking confused.

"Amy always wants to think the worst of me," he said with an exaggerated sigh. Amy didn't reply. She triumphantly pulled out a black permanent marker and turned her sign over to the blank side.

"I know what we can do to kill some time," she said, looking meaningfully at Satomi who was digging around in her own bag.

"I'm right there with you," she replied, taking out a set of markers. They were always prepared when art was involved.

Connor raised an eyebrow. "I'll chalk this up to some weird artist thing I don't understand." A loud beep echoed from the starting line, and Connor turned to look. A voice on the speaker announced that they had five minutes until the start of the race. "It's been nice seeing you two. Will you be here for the whole race?"

"At least until Arty finishes," Amy replied. "What's your training time? We'll look for you."

"Just shy of an hour and a half," he said nonchalantly. Amy's jaw dropped, but she quickly closed it.

"Well then," she said, shaking her head and sending her ponytail whipping about. "We'll be at the finish line to see if you make it." He laughed and strode away, pausing to adjust his backpack briefly. Quinton and Peter flanked him as he made his way to the front. "C'mon, Satomi, let's get to work." Holding hands to make their way through the crowd, the girls soon found an out-of-the-way space to work.

They spent a long time chatting and making the sign as elaborate as possible. It read, "WAY TO GO CONNOR!" with lots of doodles and designs on it.

Amy checked her phone. "It's been a bit over an hour. Should we go try to make our way to the finish line to see if that braggart actually ran the race that fast?" For some reason, it rankled her that Connor's training time was faster than her brother's.

Satomi gave her a sideways glance as she drew. "What's up between you two?" she asked, looking back down at her work. Amy felt her cheeks instantly heat.

"What do you mean?" she asked, trying to keep her voice neutral.

"There's something between you two. I've never seen you act like that toward anyone else before, not even Adam."

Amy snorted. "Is that what this is about?"

"I just calls 'em like I sees 'em."

Amy shrugged, then stood to stretch. "I don't know," she said as honestly as possible. "We always end up in the same place at the same time."

"So, you didn't know he would be here?" Satomi asked, capping a marker before putting it haphazardly back into her bag.

"Of course not! I didn't even know he was a runner. I wouldn't have thought it was his scene."

"If you say so." Satomi stood. "The sign looks good at least."

Amy's cheeks were still flushed as she turned away. "Let's go see if he's done." Holding hands again, they pushed through the crowd until they had a good view of the finish line. Amy scanned the incoming runners one by one, listening to the dull roar of the crowd, which was punctuated by random cheers as people crossed. Amy tugged her shirt down self-consciously, making sure it wasn't bunching up around her middle. A lot of these people were very fit-looking.

"Here he comes!" Satomi yelled before Amy felt his presence. She looked up at the clock, which showed 01:29 on it.

"You have *got* to be kidding me," she moaned. He had his jacket off and sweat was dripping off him, though his breathing was fairly even. She did her best not to notice his toned arms or how his shirt clung to his chest, instead meeting his eyes.

Satomi smacked her. "He's looking this way. Hold up the sign," she said, shoving the sign into one of Amy's hands. Together, they lifted it and began to yell and wave wildly at him. Satomi had her phone out, taking a million pictures as he ran by them. He smiled broadly, and Amy felt her cheeks heat again, and she looked away. Her eyes went unwillingly back to him, and she stared, her mouth slightly open, as he crossed the finish line. Shaking herself, she tugged Satomi over to him.

"Good job," she said, shoving the sign in his face. He laughed and pushed it back.

"Wow," he said. "You made this for me while you waited?"

"We had plenty of time," she said with a sniff. He threw back his head and laughed that deep laugh again.

"Has your brother finished yet?" he asked teasingly, his eyes crinkling. He was panting slightly and paused to wipe his forehead. Amy forced her eyes to stay on his face, idly wondering again if he'd ever let her try to draw him. He almost seemed to glow.

"Not yet," she said. "Not all of us can be freakishly fast."

He laughed. "No, I suppose we can't." He looked over as Peter and Quinton crossed the finish line, each one puffing like a bellows, looking red-faced and uncomfortable. They collapsed off to the side as soon as they crossed the line and groaned. "I suppose I'd better get those two back home to recover. They insisted on training for this and coming with me." He gave Amy a meaningful look. Connor was always being watched.

"It was good seeing you, see you at school next week." Connor waved and went over to tap the two boys with his foot, urging them upward. Amy resolutely kept from looking at him again.

"Wow. Wow. *Wow*!" Satomi gasped. "He's not my type, but that boy is *gorgeous*."

Amy shrugged, feeling the traitorous burn of her cheeks. "If you say so." Satomi elbowed her in the ribs.

"Sis, I saw you looking him up and down. You can't deny that he was sculpted by the gods themselves."

"Whatever. Let's go wait for Arty." Satomi laughed, and they held hands back through the crowd.

At the 01:43 mark, Arty, looking wiped out but exultant, crossed the finish line. Amy jumped up and down and screamed loud enough that she knew she'd have no voice the next day. She was grateful to see that Satomi had thought ahead and was taking a video of him. Amy ran after him and Satomi scrambled to follow, dragging their signs along.

"Arty, that was awesome! Did you qualify?" Amy yelled, tackling her brother as he chugged a water bottle, sending water flying all over them.

He replied, "Yes, I'll be able to run in the marathon! I'm going to the New Year's Dash Bash in January!"

"Congratulations!" Satomi burst out, finally catching up. "You did great."

"Thanks." He beamed. "I thought it would be awesome to start the new year by crushing a lifelong goal. It's not a big race and the qualifications are weird, but it's always been my dream. I'm looking forward to taking a short break from the more strenuous runs before starting some serious marathon training. I'm going to rest for a bit, then we can head home, I need a shower. I think this deserves getting takeout for lunch and ice cream for dessert."

Both girls cheered.

21

Connor

WHITTAKER HIGH WAS BUZZING WITH END-of-year energy. The students were restless, ready to be free, and the teachers had all but given up on getting them to pay attention. For the most part, students were allowed to roam the school with their yearbooks, exchanging them for signatures.

Connor had been accosted by most of his class for his signature and thus, had spent the bulk of his morning signing autographs with his normal charming smile in place, too deep into the façade to blow them off to go find Amy. He'd heard the rumors about the two of them, but he couldn't bring himself to care. He wasn't able to get away from everyone until almost lunchtime, during which he finally got to search the halls looking for his one and only best friend. Satomi was a close second now.

When he finally found her, Amy was with Satomi. They were sitting side by side in a hallway, drawing in the other's yearbook. As he approached them, Adam walked up at the same time. He squatted down and shook Amy's leg, causing her pen to slide across the page.

"Adam!" she snapped as Connor reached them. "You made me mess up!"

Adam laughed. "Hey, sorry, I just wanted to get your attention," he said, completely unabashed. Amy glared at him. "I wanted you to sign my yearb—"

"Hello, Amy," Connor said. "Will you be able to recover your art from the mistake?" She looked up at him, and he felt his breath catch momentarily when her cerulean eyes caught his as she smiled at him. Adam got a surly look on his face. She had stopped verbally throwing daggers every time she saw Connor, and Adam clearly *hated* it.

"She couldn't have messed up that badly," Adam groused.

"Mistakes happen in art, I'll incorporate it," she said, ignoring Adam.

Adam flushed. "Hey, I said I was sorry."

"It's fine, just hand me your yearbook." Adam, looking slightly mollified, handed over his book with a smile. Satomi scowled and drew a bit more aggressively in Amy's book.

Connor was pleased that she put a fraction of the effort into Adam's book that she had into Satomi's. He shook his head slightly. *What is wrong with me?* "There," she said, handing the book back. "Satomi, are you able to part from your masterpiece for a moment?"

Satomi sighed and handed over the yearbook without acknowledging Adam. "Hi, Connor," she said brightly. "Can you sign my yearbook?"

Connor was pleasantly surprised at this, a warm glow spreading through him. "Of course," he replied, giving her a half-smile. Amy handed Satomi's book to Connor while handing her own book to Adam. Each boy signed the respective book and handed them back to their owners. Connor took a bit longer because he wasn't sure what to say other than "Have a great summer." Satomi didn't ask Adam to sign her book. He liked her more and more every day.

"Don't forget to call me this summer," Adam said to Amy, standing.

"Of course," she replied, smiling.

"I'll see you later. The guys and I are going to ditch and go four-wheeling. You're welcome to join us." He turned his back slightly on Connor, making it clear he wasn't invited. Connor couldn't help a sardonic smile from spreading across his face. As if he'd be caught dead hanging out with the "Whittaker Prince." He resisted laughing at the thought of the title, seeing as he was descended from actual royalty, even if it was distantly.

"Oh, no, thank you," Amy said, shifting uncomfortably. He was not at all surprised to see she wasn't a rule breaker.

"Suit yourself, Goody-Two-Shoes. Later," he said, bumping Connor's shoulder as he walked by. Connor suppressed a grimace and the desire to turn around and smash Adam's face into a wall. The Sword's power within him tried to rush to the surface, but he shoved it down. Amy rolled her eyes.

"Sorry, Connor. He can be a bit of a jerk sometimes, but overall, he's alright." *Yeah right.* "Have a seat and sign my yearbook," Amy said, patting the ground beside her. Feeling a bit awkward, he followed her directions and took the book from her, making sure to keep several inches of space between them. A bead of sweat trickled down his back.

"Don't worry, Satomi," he said with his usual charming smile. "I'll return this to you quickly so you can finish your work."

Satomi flushed. "Oh, no problem," she stammered.

Connor opened Amy's yearbook, unsure of where to sign or what to say. He flipped through the autograph pages, noting the many generic "Have a Great Summer!" signatures. He saw the beautiful drawing of seemingly random elements that Satomi had been making. It looked like a summary of their year or perhaps, of things they shared. There were paintbrushes, lumps of clay, music notes, and so much more. He flipped to an empty page, his mind going as blank as the paper as he tried to think of what to write.

What could he say? He didn't know her well enough to have a lot to say, at least not a lot he could risk others seeing. He finally put pen to paper.

He wrote "Thank you for everything, Connor" and then stared at it for a moment. It seemed pitiful, but he couldn't think of anything else, so he closed it and handed the book back to Satomi, who immediately opened it and began to gleefully draw again.

"Would you please sign my yearbook?" Connor asked Amy politely.

"Of course." She held her hands out. He removed it from his backpack, having realized that he didn't have it out when he asked her to sign it. She giggled at him and set it on her lap, flipping through the pages. There were a ton of signatures everywhere. "Wow, Rich Boy, you sure are popular." Connor snorted. She flipped until she found an empty half page and started to draw.

Connor sat silently while both girls drew. He wasn't sure of where to look or if he should talk. He was pleased, however, that she spent a lot more time on his yearbook than on Adam's. This thought gave him pause. *Why did that matter?*

He was completely zoned out when Amy thrust his yearbook into his lap, and he jumped.

"Sorry," she said with a startled laugh. "I didn't mean to scare you, but I'm done." He looked down. Amy had sketched the park entrance and changed the sign to say, "I'm very happy that I met you. -Amy." He couldn't stop himself from smiling a real smile at the drawing. He was glad he'd shaken off Quinton and Peter earlier.

"Thank you, Amy. It's perfect." She beamed at him. "Satomi, would you also sign my yearbook?" Satomi clapped her hands excitedly as she grabbed the book without reply, finding a blank spot and starting to work.

"Do you have any fun plans for the summer?" Amy asked.

"Not really. We don't really, um, do 'fun' things in my family." Amy looked like she caught his hidden meaning and nodded. "I'll probably train and study."

"We don't usually do anything too special during the summer either. Arty wants to take a vacation, but he's always so busy—"

"I'm going to have a party this summer!" Satomi interjected excitedly. "I like to do something at the end of the summer each year, and this year, I decided on a party! Wanna come, Connor?"

His mind raced. He didn't accept invitations to class-mates' events because of the Sheath, but he found himself unable to turn down Satomi's shining face. "Of course," he said. "Just let me know when and where." He was sure he could spin it to be about staying on mission.

"Yay!" She clapped. "What's your number?" she asked, taking out her phone. Connor acquiesced, and she texted him hers.

"Can I get your number too?" Amy asked somewhat bashfully. Connor started. They had never bothered ex-changing numbers since they saw each other so often and besides, Connor was monitored by the Sheath.

"Certainly," he replied, giving it to her, and he soon heard his phone buzz as she texted him.

"How did you two not already have each other's num-bers?" Satomi asked.

"I don't know, we never thought about it," Amy said, flushing. Connor shrugged.

The end-of-day bell finally rang, and they all gathered in the bus area.

"You'll hang out with us in the summer, right, Connor?" Satomi asked hopefully.

"Of course," he replied, genuinely taken with her. Amy beamed at them.

"Hey, there's my bus!" Satomi hugged Amy quickly and, after a second of thought, she threw her arms around Connor too and then dashed away, waving backward at them.

Connor must have looked as confused as he felt because Amy laughed. "She likes you!" Connor, unsure of what to say, nodded. "I'll see you during the summer, right?" she asked, looking up at him, a slow blush creeping across her cheeks. His heart thumped in his chest a little harder.

"Naturally." Of course, it was only to get closer to her and had nothing to do with the grin threatening to spread across his face.

Her answering grin was like the sun, and Connor found himself transfixed by its warmth. He mentally shook himself. "Best friends forever," she said with a wink. Her bus rolled up. "Will you be in trouble if you come over and ditch your ride?"

Connor sighed. "Maybe. But they do like me getting close to you." She cocked her head at him. "They want me to get close to you to have a better chance at winning." He had decided a while ago that a bit of honesty would work best with her.

"Is that why you started bugging me until we became friends?" No judgment existed in her tone, but her eyes were weary. He paused, considering the question.

"Perhaps at first," he replied truthfully. "While it helped push me toward you, I didn't become your friend because of the Sheath." He hesitated, before blurting out, "It was your eyes."

"My eyes?" Amy asked, confused.

"Have a good night, Amy," he said, pushing a wild lock of hair behind her ear before he walked away.

22

Amy

After a week of relaxing, a warm summer day found Amy back in her clearing, meditating after a hard training session. She hovered in the air, eyes closed, power tightly controlled around her.

"Amy!" She opened her eyes to see Connor walking toward her, waving. *How did I not sense him?*

"Connor," she gasped as she dropped from her seat in the sky. "What are you doing here?" She walked up to him.

"I was taking my daily jog and sensed you. Did the Shield not sense me?"

"Guess I was concentrating too hard. I didn't notice you." Amy shrugged. Connor looked at her with obvious concern.

"You need to stay on guard." A frown caused a crease between his eyebrows.

"You're probably right." She shrugged again. "My shield was around me, so I wasn't in any danger."

Connor rolled his eyes. "Still..."

"Yeah, yeah," she replied, waving dismissively. "What're you doing today?"

"Today is a rare free day for me."

"Wanna spend it with me? It's about time you met Arty."

"You want me to meet your brother?" Connor asked, looking alarmed.

"Of course, we're friends now." Amy kicked at the grass. "You don't have to if you don't want to."

"It sounds fun." Connor was smiling when she looked back up at him.

"Good! Let's head over, I wanna get cleaned up." Amy turned and started walking out of the clearing.

"What's the rush?" Connor turned and stumbled slightly, but quickly regained his balance and walked beside her.

Connor, with his long legs, never had an issue keeping up with her. "We always hang out in the park, so it'll be cool to go somewhere else. When Arty gets home, we can have dinner and play games."

"It's a date," he replied with a straight face.

Amy flushed. "Stop using that phrase, it's embarrassing." Connor laughed as she shoved him.

"You're ridiculous."

"Oh, and Arty doesn't know about any of this," Amy blurted. Connor froze and Amy stopped a few steps ahead, surprised. She looked at him. "Connor?"

Connor's mouth was hanging open, and his eyes were wide. "He... doesn't know?"

She shrugged. "Nah, I don't want him to worry. Besides, he'd try to stop me."

Connor shook his head, resuming the walk. Amy wasn't sure what to say, so she changed the subject. Soon, the moment passed, and they bantered happily the whole way to Amy's apartment.

A MY CAME OUT TO THE LIVING ROOM, COMBING her slightly wet hair. Connor was sitting on the couch, browsing his phone. He'd been politely complimentary of their home again, but she was still a little embarrassed knowing how fancy his own home must be. His stance was casual, but she noticed a faint blush across his cheeks when he looked up at her and smiled.

"Welcome back," he said in a relaxed tone she didn't entirely believe.

"Sorry about that."

"For being human?"

"Um, yeah?" She stared at the ground, unsure of what to say. "So... um, do you want to play a game or something? Arty will be home in a bit and we like to play games a lot."

"Will that break the ice with your brother?" he asked as he ran a hand through his hair.

Amy opened her mouth to speak, but she paused when she heard the sound of a key being inserted into the lock. "Speak of the devil." Connor paled. "You'll be fine," she reassured him, patting his arm sympathetically.

"I'm home," Arty announced cheerfully. Connor was on his feet in an instant, his manners clearly kicking in.

"Welcome home, Arty. I'm in the living room with a friend I want you to meet."

Arty entered the room, and Amy saw Connor straighten as he flashed the charming smile she'd seen him use at school.

"Oh, hello," Arty said, walking quickly toward Connor, extending his hand. "I'm Arty. It's nice to meet you." Her stomach was suddenly heavy, and she gulped.

Connor took Arty's hand with perfect poise. "I'm Connor Callaghan. It's a pleasure to meet you as well." Cue the charming smile again.

Arty turned to Amy. "You didn't tell me your new friend was *another* boy," he teased. She groaned and put her hands over her face.

"Please don't try to do the protective big brother act, it doesn't suit you."

Arty threw his head back and laughed. "What? You already have that Adam kid around. I can't help it."

Grasping for a new subject, she asked, "Mind if Connor stays for dinner? And maybe we can play some games?" Arty's eyes lit up at the word *games* as she knew they would.

"Of course!"

Connor's stiff shoulders relaxed slightly and the pit in her stomach lightened.

"Great," she said with enthusiasm, but felt sweat suddenly break out across her forehead. *Was it a good idea to bring him here?*

"I'll go see if there's anything I can throw together in the kitchen," Arty said as he walked out of the room.

Connor stared at Amy for a moment before walking over and speaking close to her ear, keeping his voice low.

"Are you sure I should stay?" She flinched slightly at how close he was.

"Please?" she asked, looking up into his eyes. An unreadable expression crossed his face, and he sighed.

"Of course."

She beamed at him. Their eyes locked and for a moment, she was lost in the depths of his green eyes. She wanted to try to paint them. His eyes seemed to bore straight through her with their intensity. Amy felt her cheeks heat again. Could blushes become permanent?

"I guess we should see if Arty needs anything," she said, motioning Connor toward the kitchen. "Need any help, Arty?" she asked as she watched him go through the fridge.

He looked up at her, his eyes showing some fatigue. "How about we do pizza tonight? I don't know if I can deal with cooking right now. It was a long day at work." He stood and stretched his lower back with a groan.

"I think that's perfectly fair," Amy said, abandoning Connor and throwing her arms around her brother, who immediately returned her hug. She turned back to Connor, who was fidgeting with the hem of his shirt.

"I'll place the order," Arty said. He looked at Connor. "Do you have any food allergies or anything before I call?"

"No, thank you for checking."

"Why don't you pick out a game, Connor? It's only fair that the guest picks."

Connor's face flushed slightly. "I would love to."

"Great. I'll order the pizza and you two can go and pick something to play. Amy can show you where the games are." Arty took his cell phone out of his pocket and wandered off in the direction of his room.

"That could have gone worse," Amy said.

Connor barked out a laugh. "Where do you keep the games?"

"What do you like to play?" she asked, showing him to a closet in the hallway.

"You choose. I didn't play many games growing up." She frowned. "Save your pity for someone who wants it," he said sharply. Amy winced. "I'm sorry, that was out of line."

She opened her mouth to speak, but Arty chose that moment to come back.

"Did you choose?" he asked.

"I thought we'd go with an oldie," Amy said, ripping her eyes away from Connor. She wasn't sure she could look at him anymore.

She grabbed The Game of Life and placed it on the coffee table in the living room. Arty sat on the couch while Amy and Connor sat side by side on the ground, each careful not to let their legs touch. "It's a classic," Amy told Connor, giving him a small smile, trying to tell him without words that she was okay. Looking at Arty, she said, "Connor didn't play a lot of games growing up."

Arty placed a hand on his chest in mock horror, gasped loudly, and contorted his face in an exaggerated display of shock. "*What*? The uncultured swine!" Connor snorted. The rich boy had probably never been called uncultured before. "We can't have that. We'll take you through all the classics. You'll be a game aficionado by the time we're through with you," Arty concluded.

The night was one of the most fun, yet awkward, Amy had ever had. Connor never fully relaxed, but he definitely seemed much looser by dark when he'd had to excuse himself.

"You can come over anytime, Connor," Arty said with a smile, stretching. "This was a lot of fun. Need a ride home?"

Connor paused. "That's okay. I'll walk over to the park and have a car pick me up."

Arty frowned. "I'd feel better if we drove you over there." He didn't ask why it had to be at the park. Arty was cool like that.

"No, that's okay," he said, waving off Arty's suggestion. "I'll be fine."

"I can walk you there?" Amy asked, not ready for the night to end.

"It's dark," Arty interjected, looking sternly at her.

"C'mon, I walk there all the time."

"I can have my chauffeur drop her off nearby," Connor suggested.

Arty sighed in defeat. "Be back soon," he said sternly. "And stick together." He didn't comment on Connor having a chauffeur either.

"Will do!" Amy exclaimed, hugging her brother tightly. "Let's go," she said, bounding out the door, followed closely by Connor.

"Good night, Arty. Thank you for dinner, it was a pleasure meeting you," Connor said politely, his hand on the doorknob.

"You too," Arty said, waving. Connor closed the door and turned to Amy who began to lead them down the stairs and toward the park automatically. They walked in silence for a minute, Connor slightly ahead.

"Tonight was fun," he said, not looking at her.

"Do you want to come over again sometime?"

"Of course," he replied, then slowed to match her pace. "I had a lot of fun. Your brother is pretty cool."

"Isn't he the best?" she said. "Today was awesome." She sighed happily.

"Today was the best."

After too short of a time, they reached the park entrance and Connor let out a long sigh.

"Hey," Amy said, looking up into his face with concern. "You okay?"

"Yes. I just need to get back into character."

"Character?"

"I need to be the me that my family knows. I tend to let my guard down around you because I can't help myself." He smiled ruefully.

"Is that why you didn't want us to drop you off at your house?" she asked.

"Yes, and why I'll have Roland drop you off near, but not at, your apartment."

"That makes sense. The Sheath probably aren't the nicest, huh?"

"No, they are not."

Amy felt a pang at his words. She had Arty, and she knew that her parents had loved her very much. Connor didn't have anyone. "Are you all alone?" she asked sadly. He looked down at her, then looked away quickly.

"No. I'm close to our butler Bertram, but he's the only one." He took out his phone. "I'm going to call Roland now." He put the phone to his ear, said where he was, and immediately hung up.

"Wow, rude," she admonished, smacking his arm.

"I told you, I have to be in character. I haven't told them that you know I'm the Sword, so I'll act a little differently toward you, but it'll be okay. Just be yourself."

"Okay..." Amy fidgeted, suddenly nervous, and they lapsed into a familiar, awkward silence. It happened often enough that she almost found it comforting.

Finally, the car rolled up, and Amy saw Connor's face transform into the cool, detached look she'd seen him wear at school. When the car stopped, she reached for the handle but paused when she heard the driver's side door open. She looked up, confused.

A tall man in a black suit got out and hurried around the car. Amy watched as he opened the door for her, hands clutched in front of her chest. "Please, Miss," the man said in a deep voice, "have a seat." If he thought there was anything weird about her being there, he kept it to himself.

She hesitantly entered the car and made room for Connor. Connor got in without acknowledging the driver, who immediately closed the door and ran back to the front. Amy glanced around, uncomfortably aware of how fancy the interior was. She clasped her hands on her lap and looked down, resisting the urge to fidget more.

"Roland, bring us to the corner of 9th and Stewart," Connor ordered. "Amy needs to go home, and I would prefer not to make her walk." She tried hard to hide her shock at his cool tone, unused to seeing this side of him. Connor's eyes darted over to her before looking straight ahead again.

Amy kept her mouth shut—she was a terrible actress, and she knew it, and she had no idea how to act here. She was poorly suited for any kind of intrigue, whereas Connor seemed to wear it like a second skin. That thought made her even more uncomfortable, and she rubbed her hands together.

Connor didn't even glance at her. He kept his gaze coolly ahead and his expression blank. "Amy, would you like to hang out again sometime soon?" he asked, his tone charming and polite as he looked down at her with a dazzling smile. She recognized it as one that he used at school to beguile everyone around him. She wanted to roll her eyes at him but resisted.

"That'd be great," she replied, trying to sound enthusiastic but, judging by the slight wince on Connor's face, didn't do a good job. This was why she avoided any kind of drama class and preferred to help the theater kids with their sets.

After approximately one thousand years, the car pulled up to a grocery store. Amy moved to exit, but Connor grabbed her arm. She flinched, looking up at him in surprise.

"Wait," he said gruffly, and she froze. Roland got out and came around to her door, then opened it. Resisting the urge to leap from the car, she exited gracefully, smiling up at Roland.

"Thank you for the ride," she said.

"It was no problem, Miss," he replied with a nod, looking bit abashed.

She bent down to look into the car. "I'll see you later, Connor."

"Have a good evening," he replied, nodding at her with a hint of a smile. Amy walked toward a nearby apartment, but not her own. Her legs screamed at her to run, but she stopped herself. She would never, ever ride anywhere with Connor again. When the car was out of sight, she let out a breath before she jogged toward her actual home.

She flung the door open and just about flew into the entrance.

"Everything okay?" Arty asked, popping his head out of his room. Amy walked into the living room and threw herself onto the couch.

"It was *sooooo* awkward. That was the most awkward drive I have ever been on." She threw an arm over her eyes.

"Really? The *most* awkward?" Arty asked, entering the living room. "Even considering who you have as a brother?"

"The. *Most.*"

"What was so awkward?"

"This is the most complicated relationship I have ever had." Amy ignored Arty's garbled sound at the word *relationship*. "It's like he's in a totally different world. Sure, Adam is a rich boy too, but Connor is on a whole other level."

"When you say... 'relationship'..." Arty sounded like someone was strangling him. Amy groaned and threw a couch pillow across the room at him.

"Not you too!" she half shouted. "Ugh, you and Satomi. If you both had your way, I'd be married off by now."

"*God* no." He gagged. "I just want to keep ahead of things. You know, we should probably have a talk about—"

"No. He's just a friend who's a boy," she choked, shooting upright with cheeks ablaze. "We will *not* be having that talk now or ever. I went to health class." Arty chuckled, his pale cheeks a vibrant shade of red. "But you like him?"

"I do," he said. "He seems like a good kid."

"He is," she agreed. "Though completely uncultured."

23
Amy

AMY SLEPT IN, WAKING UP LONG AFTER ARTY had left for work, having to work on the weekend for a big project. She shambled like a zombie to the kitchen, still half asleep. The beige carpeting of the hallway was scratchy on the soles of her feet, and she realized she'd forgotten to put on slippers.

"*Good morning, Amy.*" The familiar voice of the Shield rang in her brain. Amy became immediately encased in a glowing orb with a ball of energy in her hand, ready to be thrown. Her heartbeat pounded in her ears. "*Excellent re-flexes. I'm glad to see you haven't been slacking in my... forced absence.*"

Amy realized that she'd become accustomed to being alone in her mind and wasn't sure when the spirit had dug its way out of the prison she'd buried it in. She released the energy around her and settled onto the ground.

"What do you want?" she snapped, continuing to the kitchen. With Arty gone, she answered the spirit out loud.

"*I have thought about it, and I decided to allow your misguided friendship with the Sword host to continue.*"

"*Allow?*" Amy demanded. "You're training me to die like fattened up livestock and think you can tell me what I can and can't do while I'm still alive?"

The spirit paused. "*Die?*"

"When you exit my body, I'll die," Amy said simply. She could almost feel the Shield thinking.

"*Did Connor tell you this?*"

"Yeah."

"*And you believe him?*"

"I do."

"*He is not wrong,*" she said at last. "*I preferred to not tell you, but to my knowledge, every host has died after the battle was over. It could be due to the strain of the battle, or from injuries. I would imagine that my leaving your body would be catastrophic, but I was not around once the battle was over to confirm.*"

"You *preferred* not to tell me?" Amy hissed.

"*I thought it would be kinder for you to be allowed to hope. Living beings crave hope.*"

Amy's power burned brightly. With a deep breath, she called it back and floated effortlessly to the ground once more.

"*Your control has improved dramatically.*"

"No thanks to you."

"*Regardless, your guided training needs to continue. You cannot improve fast enough without my assistance.*"

"I'd rather drink poison. Same outcome, easier path."

"I will... attempt to be less formal and more open with you. You are... very spirited—"

She choked out a laugh, interrupting the spirit. "Ha! I'm *spirit*ed? What a terrible pun."

The spirit paused again. *"That was an awful pun. I did not mean to make it."*

Amy doubled over, tears streaming down her face as laughter overtook her. "Finally," she said. "Do you *promise* to be nicer and to not give me grief for being Connor's friend?" She wiped her eyes, stomach aching.

"I think that it is unwise, but if it is what I must do, I will overlook it."

"How magnanimous." Amy rolled her eyes. "You wanna meet him? Maybe be more aware when I'm around him instead of skulking away?"

"Perhaps."

"He didn't have a choice in this anymore than I did. We're both possessed by you things, and we're both going to die. He's my friend. You have to accept that."

She heard the spirit sigh in defeat. *"Very well. Arrange a meeting and I will observe the Sword boy."*

"I would also like an apology."

"Yes, yes. I apologize for calling you names and hiding the truth. It was impolite and wrong of me. Would you like to go to the park?" the spirit asked, changing the subject.

"Sure. I need to eat and clean up first, I just woke up."

Without speaking further, she felt the spirit's presence recede. She took a long shower and ate breakfast, taking her time. Her favorite veggie breakfast sausages didn't taste quite as good as normal today. As she strolled leisurely toward the park, her phone dinged. She lit up when she saw it was a text from Connor.

Connor: Sorry if last night was weird.

Amy: It was okay.

Amy: I'm going to the park.
Wanna meet me in a few hours?

Amy entered the park. She looked lovingly at the sun streaming through the trees around her and inhaled the fresh air. Smiling at the distant sound of children playing somewhere out of sight, she meandered down the paths, taking her time before finding her usual clearing.

Connor: Sure.

"I'm here!" she declared within her mind, skipping in. *"I invited Connor to meet us in a few hours."*

"Fine. Today we will be focusing on physical self-defense. I will be teaching you to fight without your powers." Amy wasn't sure if she was excited or terrified.

She stepped forward hesitantly, unsure how this would work.

They spent the next hour going over proper form for fighting and how to get out of holds. Amy learned how to throw a punch somewhat properly, but she also learned that using her elbows was better. The spirit showed her what to do in her mind like she was watching a movie. The information was channeled directly into her, an indescribable sensation. Her muscles now had memories she didn't.

"We won't spend much time on this, but it is very important that you learn these things."

"Connor's been training his whole life, so I don't know how much of a difference it'll make." She panted and flopped backward onto the ground.

"I heard my name?" Connor said as he entered the clearing. Amy felt the Shield tense within her and sighed.

"Hey, Connor," she said from the ground. "I've been learning self-defense. I said that you could kick my butt without even trying." She groaned and closed her eyes.

"Ah, you're not wrong." He looked around. "Have you... been being trained by your spirit... directly?"

"Yep. I don't have anyone else that can do it."

Connor looked slightly uncomfortable, scuffing his foot on the ground. "What would you like to do today?"

"I'm not sure. We could go to my house and play games again or go on the swings, maybe."

"I don't think I've ever gone on the swings," he replied. He thought a moment longer as Amy stared up at him with her mouth hanging open. "No, wait, I have. When I was very young, I remember Bertram taking me to a park when my parents were out." He smiled warmly.

"Let's go swing then," she said, springing up excitedly. He flinched slightly, but didn't object. They walked toward the playground, which turned out to be empty. "How unusual," she remarked, immediately sitting on a swing. "Maybe there was an event in town." Connor sat on the swing next to her while she pumped her legs. Connor started slower.

"Bertram always pushed me," he remarked, finally swinging as high as Amy after watching her.

"Bertram sounds like a great guy."

"He is. Father is my biological father, but I would say that Bertram is the person I think of most as a dad."

"Does he know about this side of you?" she asked, glancing over at him. His hair was blowing in the breeze, and he looked like he was in the middle of some kind of photoshoot. Her cheeks burned, and she looked away quickly.

"To an extent. He has known me since birth and sees that I am not the same as my father."

Amy interrupted the sudden tension with a question. "Can our powers do anything fun?"

Connor looked at her. "More fun than flying?"

"Flying is a bit hard to hide, but I thought my heart was going to burst the first time I ever flew."

"Hmm... what about making things?"

"Making things?"

"Yeah." He looked around and then held out a hand. A stream of gray light shot out and created a cushion shape about five feet in front of him. He swung as high as he could and, using his power, launched himself onto the cushion.

"I've never made something away from me that wasn't a blast of energy to throw!" Amy exclaimed. She held out a hand like Connor had and sent energy in front of her. Sweat formed on her forehead as she made a blob shape and then launched herself at it, praying it would catch her. She landed on it, and it stopped her, but it popped and dropped her to the ground. "Oof!"

"Are you alright?" he asked, humor and concern mingling in his voice as he jogged over to her after gliding gracefully to the ground.

"Yep." Amy sat up and put both hands out, creating a bubble in front of her. She concentrated and made it more of a squashed bean bag shape before standing up and flopping onto it. "Shield chic." Connor created a cube before shaping it into a sort of armchair and taking a seat. "Show off," she grumbled. He smirked. She looked up and saw the sun was lowering in the sky. "I should probably head home before it gets dark, but I'm not accepting a ride from you again."

"That's fair," Connor said as he popped his armchair. Amy did the same with less grace and then they walked toward the Northern entrance. "Have you spoken to Satomi this summer?"

"We text almost every day. She got home from Japan a while back, and we're going to the movies soon."

"That sounds nice. And Adam?" He looked straight ahead, face neutral.

Amy looked up at him, crinkling her nose. "Like you care how Adam is doing," she said dryly. He chuckled.

"I don't particularly care for him, but I was asking because you're my friend, and I was curious."

She raised an eyebrow at him, but he maintained a completely innocent expression as he looked straight ahead. "He's texted me randomly and has invited me out a few times. We're going to see a movie later this summer, but that's about it. There isn't a whole lot to do around here, and I don't usually go on the vacations he invites me to."

"Vacations?" Connor frowned slightly, his eyebrows drawing together.

"Yeah. His parents like to travel a lot, so he spends a lot of time in the summer out of town. Sometimes he invites me, but I don't know his family super well, so I don't go."

"Huh."

"What about you? Does your family travel?"

"Sometimes for work, but not really for vacations, at least not as a family. Do you and Arty ever go on vacation?"

"Every now and again we'll go out of state to see new things, but he doesn't usually have a lot of time off to go do things. We're more the homebody types anyway."

"It must be nice to like being home." It was like ice water had been splashed over her. "I'm sorry, I shouldn't have blurted that out. Forget it."

Amy wasn't sure what to say so she said nothing as she followed him down a path.

24

Amy

HEY AMES. YOU EXCITED FOR THE MOVIE?"
Amy came down the stairs of her apartment to see a smiling Adam standing beside his white SUV, his normal haughtiness completely gone from his face. She nodded and ran over to give him a quick hug before climbing into his car.

"I haven't seen you in weeks, how've you been?" Amy asked as she clung to the door's handle. Adam's driving left something to be desired.

"Not too bad, just traveling and stuff," he replied, a frown tugging down the corner of his mouth. Amy waited for him to elaborate. He sighed. "It's just been kind of stressful, you know?" He ran a hand through his hair, unknowingly mimicking Connor. "My family keeps making me learn more about the different businesses, but I don't know if that's what I want."

This was a topic they'd spoken of at length. "Have you told them that yet?"

He sighed again, louder this time. "No. How can I tell them I wanna leave the town that our family started? It's not like I have any siblings to pass the burden off to." His frown deepened.

"Are they still at least encouraging college?"

"Yeah, but they want me to get an MBA at the closest state one so I can be nearby. I can't even choose my own major."

"Do you know where you'd want to go if you could choose anywhere?" Amy thunked into the door as he took a corner a little too sharply.

"No, I just know I want to go somewhere else. Maybe out of state." He took another sharp turn. "It must be nice to know exactly what you want." He gave her a small smile as he glanced over at her. *Keep your eyes on the road!* She worked to keep her face from showing how much she hated his driving.

"Kind of. I don't know exactly what I want to do after school, though. Just a general hope of being an in demand graphic designer."

Adam snorted. "There's no way you won't get into Clearwater and then be super in demand with your talent. If I do take over the family business, I'll hire you myself."

"That would be something," Amy said, feeling heat touch her cheeks. *I don't know about that.* "What do you want to major in?"

For a minute, only the radio playing pop music could be heard as he thought, and Amy hummed along. "Honestly? I want to try a bunch of different things. I've never been able to really pursue anything I want, you know? It'd be fun to try a ton of things and see what I like."

"That would be a lot of fun, I think you should talk to your folks about it. They love you, I'm sure they'd want you to be happy."

"I think they'd rather me be miserable than ever besmirch the Whittaker name." Amy grimaced, thinking how similar Connor and Adam's family situations were. She almost laughed thinking of how much they'd hate to hear that, quickly schooling her face back into one of concern.

"You won't know until you try."

"Yeah, maybe." His tone made it clear that he didn't want to talk about it anymore.

They pulled into the Barrington Mall parking garage, walked to the theater, and Adam scanned his phone at the kiosk before they made their way to the concessions, the smell of popcorn overpowering. Amy's mouth watered.

"I'm paying for food to repay the ticket," Amy said, pulling out her wallet as they approached.

"If you want," he said, gesturing her forward. They ordered and went to find their seats. They sat down and both began to happily munch on popcorn and chocolate candies, sipping sodas. "I really like that you do that," Adam said, his words garbled around a mouthful of popcorn.

Amy laughed quietly, the previews not quite starting yet. "Do what?"

"Don't make me pay for everything."

"Well yeah. Why would I?" She mixed chocolates and popcorn in her mouth, thoroughly enjoying the sweetness of the candy mixing with the salty popcorn. Before Adam could reply, the previews started and they were distracted by all the new movies coming out in the fall, exchanging excited whispers about which they hoped to be able to see at some point.

As they walked back to the car, Amy exclaimed, "Could you believe how wild that fight sequence was? He took on like five guys at once!"

"Right? I can't wait for *Code of Retribution Three*!"

"You think there'll be a third one?" Amy asked, climbing into the car.

"Oh yeah. They make way too much money off this franchise to stop adding to it."

The rest of the car ride was spent meticulously comparing the first and second movies in the series. As they pulled up to Amy's apartment, Adam said, "This was really fun, Ames. I appreciate that you just let me be... me when we're together." He parked the car close to the base of the stairs.

Amy smiled at him. "Of course. What are best friends for?"

Adam's face froze. "Yep, best friends forever," he replied, giving her a thumbs up. "I'm sorry I can't hang longer, I have plans this evening."

"No problem, this was a lot of fun," Amy said as she got out of the car and turned to wave at him. "Have a good night, Adam."

"Night Ames."

25
Amy

O w!" AMY YELLED, CLUTCHING HER CHEEK. "Dude, you can't get me in the face!" She rubbed at the growing red spot. "Is this gonna bruise? It's gonna bruise, isn't it?"

The Shield had taken advantage of Amy's distracted mind and hit her in the face with a training dummy, knocking her down. Satomi's "End of Summer Bash" was that week, and Satomi had included Connor on the invite list. Amy's stomach knotted whenever she thought of the stares they'd get.

"I tried not to hit you very hard. I merely wanted to show you that your guard was down. You need to focus in a fight."

"Yeah, yeah, I know." She stood and stretched, her muscles screaming at her. "I'm gonna have to take a break for the next week or so, I don't want to show up with weird bruises at the party. We can train on energy manipulation instead."

The spirit thought about it for a moment. "*That would be wise. If you have not told your friends that you are training in self-defense, it would be strange if you looked beat up.*" The spirit had long since given up on trying to get Amy to ignore her "normal" life as long as she kept training.

"Are we done?"

"*We are. Please do your stretches. We will reconvene tomorrow.*" Amy felt the spirit recede to the back of her mind.

As Amy stretched, she let her mind wander. Training and having powers were kind of cool, but the nagging sense of dread over her impending doom sometimes woke her up in the middle of the night. She'd wake up shaking and covered in cold sweat. It was easy to distract herself during the daytime, but not when she was alone or asleep. She breathed deeply, working to control the anxiety.

Leaning back on her hands, she looked up at the sky, grounding herself by enjoying the cool breeze across her skin and the feeling of the grass beneath her hands. As she debated the shape of a cloud, she sensed Connor approaching.

"Hello, Amy." He stopped and looked closer at her. "What happened to your face?" She looked at him in surprise and thought she saw a flash of anger cross his expression.

"Oh, this?" she said, quickly covering her cheek and trying to downplay it. "I wasn't paying attention."

"Paying attention?" He looked around, confused. "To what?"

"The Shield. It's been able to control some shapes outside of me, like training dummies. I wasn't paying attention and *bam*, right in the kisser." She laughed, but Connor didn't. He was staring, transfixed, at the red mark. His eyes narrowed slightly, and his breathing became erratic.

Amy's laughter died away as he continued staring at the mark. She reached out with her senses, and his energy was all over the place. His eyes flickered black while dark energy crackled around him. A bubble of gold appeared around Amy instinctively, causing her to flinch, and she stood with her hands held out. Her heart pounded and goose bumps rippled up her arms.

"Connor!" she yelled. "Connor, calm down. The Sword is preying on whatever you're feeling, and you're losing control. You need to take a deep breath and find your cen—" Before she could finish, a ball of brilliant gray light slammed into her shield. She looked at his distorted face. He was losing control. The Shield's power roiled inside of her, and nausea crept up her throat.

Breathing deeply, she dropped her shield and stared up at the gray mass before her. Connor lunged for her, but she swiped a hand and created a barrier, which he slammed a glowing fist into, bouncing backward. He wrung his hand, and Amy swore she heard him growl.

"Connor," she said again. "It's me, not the Shield. Shove the Sword down. It's not time for us to die." The truth of her words resonated in her soul. He came at her again, but this time, she grabbed his arm and used his momentum to fling him behind her. She was too small to pin him like this, so she got him behind the knees and sent him sprawling. She leapt onto his back and put him in a chokehold. "Connor," she said in his ear. "Breathe." She realized the irony of telling him to breathe while half choking him, but she couldn't afford to give up her advantage. His rage was making him an easy opponent.

His breaths came out in hard gasps. She wasn't applying enough pressure to cut off his airway completely. After several tense minutes, the dark light faded back into him, and he relaxed. Finally, she sensed almost no energy coming from him and released him, his head smacking into the grass. She fell to her knees beside him, trembling as exhaustion swamped her.

"My apologies," he gasped, clutching his head.

"You okay?" she asked, scared to go near him lest her power aggravate his. "What happened?"

"I'll be fine, I just haven't lost control in a long time." He rolled onto his back, wincing. They both stayed on the ground, their ragged breathing the only sound for several long minutes.

"What happened?" she asked again. Connor covered his face with his hands.

"I... I don't know. It was very sudden."

Amy looked at him thoughtfully as he continued to breathe deeply. He kept his face covered, refusing to look at her. "You're lying," she said. Connor stiffened, but he remained quiet. She waited a beat before continuing. "You're lying," she said again. "You lost control when you saw my face." He still didn't respond or look at her, but his cheeks started to turn red. Amy smiled softly at him, running her fingers through the grass. "Are you going to Satomi's party? She told me she invited you."

He peeked up at her. "Is it alright if I go? I know you don't want the rumor mill to spin."

"Screw the rumor mill," Amy said. "You're my friend. Let people say whatever they want."

"I'll go then." He went back to covering his eyes and taking deep, even breaths.

Amy did a few yoga poses as Connor recovered. When she'd finished all of her stretches, she curled up on the ground beside him. They stayed in comfortable silence for a while longer before Connor stirred. He sat up and stretched, looking over at her.

"I'm sorry for wasting the whole evening," he said at last.

"Hey, I've been there. I missed school when I first lost control and slept for an entire day."

He stood and she followed suit. "Thanks for staying with me."

"You'd have done the same."

"Shall we head home?"

"Sure." They walked in silence on opposite sides of the path, Amy trying to think of different reasons why Connor would lose control but coming up empty. Once they were about halfway to the entrance, she broke the silence. "Do you want to talk about it?"

Connor stiffened and ran both hands through his hair. "Not really."

"Why did you lose control?"

He let out a frustrated sigh and messed his hair up even further. "I said I don't know."

"And I said you're lying."

He rounded on her, throwing his hands out wide. "And what if I am?" he shouted. She looked at him, keeping her face as expressionless as possible, and waited. Their gazes stayed locked until Connor finally turned and started walking again. Amy had to jog to keep up with his long strides, grabbing his arm. He yanked it away and glared at her. "Knock it off."

"No. Why are you lying?"

"Because it doesn't make sense!" he yelled. "I saw your face and I just snapped, okay? It's not fair that you, of all people, have to do this. None of this is fair." He rubbed a hand down his face. "I don't really know what I was thinking, okay?"

Amy wrapped her arms around him for a brief second, letting go before he even had a chance to return the hug. "It's okay, Connor. I understand. I'll see you at the party. Good night." She left him on the path and finished her walk home alone.

26
Connor

SATOMI'S "END OF SUMMER PARTY BASH-TACULAR" was in the late afternoon, and Connor had been in his closet for the better part of twenty minutes trying to figure out what to wear. *How do normal people dress to attend park gatherings? What is a "bash-tacular?" Would it be weird to call Amy and ask?*

He decided to dress as if he was going to school. Most of his clothes were neutral and tailored anyway, so one outfit was fairly similar to the next. His stomach fluttered, as if he'd swallowed moths, when he stepped out of his room. He walked with an even pace toward the main garage, keeping his face a mask and affixing a slight sneer.

"Connor, where are you going?" *Dang it.* Of *course* he'd be seen.

"To continue my mission with the Shield girl," he replied as curtly as possible as he turned to face his father, who looked at him for several long seconds. Sweat trickled down his back, but he held his father's gaze.

"Are you entirely certain you're not spending too much time with this girl?"

"What could be a better use of my time than weakening the Shield?"

Preston threw back his head and let out a hideous laugh.

"Excellent. Do not disappoint me." Preston walked on, not waiting for a response. Connor resisted the urge to let out a sigh of relief as he proceeded to his car. He didn't want attendants today.

The closer he got to Amy's apartment, the lighter he felt. It had always been a confusing sensation, but he enjoyed how he felt when they were together—confusion and all.

He parked and walked toward the entrance. When he reached the bottom of the stairs, he froze. Should he go up and surprise her? Would waiting down here be weird? What would a normal person do? He paced, then leaned against a wall.

Okay, Connor, think. What should—

"Connor!" Amy bounded toward him, her blue eyes captivating him instantly, as always. She was dressed nicer than usual with a light touch of makeup, and his mouth went dry as he took her in. Amy blushed, and he quickly shook himself out of his stupor.

"I thought I would escort you to the party," he said, standing up straight. Amy regarded him thoughtfully. "Too weird?"

"Not really. I did say to screw the rumor mill after all." Amy looped her arm with his and pulled him in the direction of the park. He was slightly taken aback by the casual contact but didn't mind it. He matched his pace to her shorter one.

"So, what happens at these things?" he asked, unable to help himself. "I don't usually attend these kinds of gatherings."

"Oh, you know, we all get drunk and then throw rocks at people. It's great," she replied dryly. He paused and looked at her with a raised eyebrow. She snorted. "We hang out, talk, eat, and maybe play some games. It's very casual and fun."

"You're weird."

"Your face is weird," she countered. He laughed. These surprise belly laughs were not unpleasant. Amy skipped ahead, releasing him in her excitement. "Will it really be weird if we show up at the same time?" she wondered out loud, looking at him.

"Weird like my face?" he teased, smiling. He could not possibly care less what the people of the town thought of him. At least not as long as it didn't interfere with his mission.

"Careful, Connor. People will start to think you're not a complete jerk," she teased back. They walked through the entrance and saw the party in the covered area. It was hard to miss all the colors at any distance.

"Amy!" Satomi's voice rang from across the field. Amy's face broke into a grin as she spun around and sprinted toward her. The two met in the middle for a massive hug. Connor looked away, choosing instead to look at the party setup as he walked toward them.

Satomi threw herself at him for a fierce hug. He patted

her back awkwardly, unsure of what to do with his arms. Amy barely suppressed a giggle, and he rolled his eyes at her.

"You're here!" Satomi released him and danced around. "I'm so excited! Come on, there's plenty to eat. I need to finish setting up a few more things." Amy and Connor followed behind Satomi who led them to a wildly decorated covered area. Satomi's parents were at the grill, getting it started. Connor noted Satomi's mother was painfully plain in contrast with her wild, neon bedecked daughter while her father dressed more like Satomi, though less colorful. Satomi climbed onto a wobbling folding chair to finish pinning up streamers, standing on her tiptoes.

"Please, let me do that," he said, looking at the precariously perched girl. It would probably ruin things if she fell, and he needed this time away.

Satomi eyed him. "I suppose you're taller," she conceded, getting off the chair. Connor took her place and pinned up the streamers, mimicking how he saw the others placed, as he'd never hung streamers before.

People were filtering in and soon, the air was thick with the sounds of laughter and chatter. Satomi was in her element, socializing with anyone and everyone, looking like a literal butterfly with the way she flitted from person to person. Amy, on the other hand, seemed to stay out of the center of attention. Connor had his full charming persona on display but stayed near her. He superficially charmed everyone that talked to him. It was exhausting.

After about an hour, the general consensus was that it was time to play frisbee. Everyone interested in playing stood around and casually threw the frisbee to each other while they talked. The atmosphere was happy and relaxed as friends who hadn't seen each other in months reconnected. Connor was relaxing into himself, feeling less robotic than normal.

"Heeeey!" a boisterous voice yelled.

So much for relaxing.

Adam walked up to the party, waving. Amy turned to look at him right as a frisbee sailed toward her head. Connor jumped in front of her and caught the frisbee, sending it soaring to the next person. He winked at her and saw her blush as he returned to her side in the circle as people cheered his reflexes. Connor saw Adam's smile falter, and he felt a little lighter.

"Hey, Adam!" Amy called back, waving exuberantly. Connor could almost hear Satomi rolling her eyes and resisted the urge to roll his own. Adam jogged over to her and gave her a big bear hug, glaring at Connor over her shoulder. Connor kept his expression neutral, and his eyes focused on the game.

Never let the enemy know you care.

"You wanna join?" Amy asked Adam politely as he set her down.

"Sure," Adam said, taking a spot between Amy and Connor.

Adam caught every frisbee aimed toward Connor, who bore it with good grace. Amy, on the other hand, did not. She started to wing the frisbee behind Adam to Connor, who caught it with a wicked grin each time before sending it across the circle, which clearly enraged Adam. He tried to keep a friendly look on his face, but his cheeks were turning a mottled red with his repressed rage.

"This is getting boring," said a kid across the circle. "Let's go eat." There were murmurs of agreement, and the game was dropped as people headed back to the tables. Connor walked to Amy's side, but Adam shouldered his way between them. The Sword's power swirled lightly in Connor's core, and he took a few deep breaths through his nose to calm himself.

"How've you been?" Adam asked Amy, keeping Connor slightly behind him. Connor toyed with the idea of tripping Adam with his powers but decided against it. What if someone saw? Besides, getting along with Amy's friends was paramount to getting along with her, his mission.

"I've been good, nothing exciting since the last time I saw you. I'm just dreading going back to school," she replied. "How about you? Have you done anything fun? It's been a week or two since we last talked."

"Yeah, we took a cruise to the Bahamas, which was awesome, and spent a lot of time on the boat."

"That sounds like a blast," Amy said. Connor couldn't tell if she was being serious or not. He decided she probably was, because she was far too nice for this imbecile.

"It was! It would have been more fun if you could have joined."

Connor involuntarily rolled his eyes. He wanted to gag.

"I told you, I don't have a passport, and I've been busy. I'm glad you had fun though."

They made it back to the tables for another round of hotdogs and hamburgers—Satomi made sure to have all different types for everyone's dietary needs, and Connor was pleased to be able to have a leaner turkey dog while Amy took a tofu one. Adam was still chatting with Amy, so

Connor decided to go sit by Satomi. He didn't trust himself not to cause a scene, and if there was one thing the Sheath hated, it was being noticed.

"This has been a lot of fun," he said as he sat beside her.

Satomi beamed up at him. "Hasn't it been a blast? I love doing this sort of thing." He watched her scarf down a hotdog and noted dryly that her manners had not improved in the months since he'd last seen her. It didn't bother him nearly as much as it had before though.

"I can tell you're quite the party planner."

"I like being around a lot of people, though I wasn't expecting Adam. Has he been behaving at least?" she asked with a hint of disgust.

"He's been tolerable," Connor replied, picking up his hotdog and delicately biting into it. This kind of food was strange to him, but he found it enjoyable.

"I hate that guy," she said grumpily. "I didn't invite him." She bit fiercely into her own hotdog.

"I'm not a big fan either," he admitted. "But you can't really invite your whole class without him showing up."

"True," Satomi admitted. "But I'm glad you're here. You two dating yet?" Connor choked on his food, and Satomi pounded his back, laughing, while he coughed.

"We're just friends," he choked out at last, reaching for a water bottle.

"Whatever you say," she said slyly. "But her eyes don't light up like that for Adam."

Connor did his absolute best not to blush at her ridiculous statement. He looked over and saw Adam stand up and start walking toward him and Satomi, and he suppressed a sigh.

"Hey, Satomi," Adam said cordially, using his shoulder to bump Connor aside on the bench. Connor felt the Sword bubbling beneath his skin but held it back as the interloper joined them. Imagining throwing Adam across the table eased his irritation a bit.

"Hello, Adam," Satomi replied with obviously forced cheer.

"Great party you have here."

"Yeah, it's been a lot of fun."

Connor glanced over to see Amy watching them closely.

"So why wasn't I invited?" Adam asked.

"I didn't get a chance to see you," she answered smoothly. Connor admired her tact. She may have terrible table manners, but she was an expert at handling people.

Adam turned his gaze toward Connor almost unwillingly. "How have you been, Connor?"

"Well, thank you. And yourself?"

"Good, good." An awkward silence ensued. "So, you've spent the summer here, then? No traveling?"

"No, I preferred staying here this summer."

"With Amy?"

"We hung out," Connor replied. Satomi flittered off to a different group as soon as the tension in the air ratcheted up.

"Are you interested in her?" Adam had decided to take the direct approach, it seemed.

"I am interested in her happiness," Connor said dryly. *What am I supposed to say to that?*

"Back off," Adam said. "I saw her first."

"I didn't realize she was a thing." He kept his anger and

power in check by idly imagining slamming Adam's head onto the picnic table.

"Adam? Connor?" Amy called, her tone weary. She walked purposefully toward them, seemingly intent on breaking up anything brewing.

"Oh, hey, Ames," Adam said. "We were talking sports." She crossed her arms and cocked a hip out, raising an eyebrow.

"Sports?" she asked disbelievingly, those blue eyes of hers flashing.

"Yes," Connor said. "Sometimes, things get rather heated when people discuss sports." Adam shot a glare at Connor.

"I need to head out," Adam said shortly. "I'll see you guys at school." With that, he stood and left, bumping Connor's shoulder with his own for the one-millionth time.

"If he does that one more time, I am going to break him," Connor muttered.

"But thank you for not," Amy said, putting a hand on his shoulder and smiling shyly at him. "I swear, Adam can be a great guy. His head gets swollen, and he gets so overwhelmed with everyone's expectations that he lashes out."

"You really see the best in everyone, don't you?"

"I guess. I did see something in you," she teased.

"See? You're too kind for this world."

"Nah," she said dismissively. "The world needs people who believe in the goodness of others."

"I'll believe in your goodness," he replied, catching her eye. "I'll leave the rest of the world up to you." For a moment, they stayed locked in place, staring at each other.

"Whatever," she said, breaking eye contact. "Let's go see Satomi." He gave a half-smile.

As the sun began to set, people started to drift away and soon, only Amy and Connor were left helping Satomi and her family finish cleaning up.

"This was the best day!" Satomi declared happily.

"I'll say," Amy said just as happily, taking down the last of the streamers.

"Thank you for not taking Adam's bait," Satomi said while wrapping Connor in a huge hug. He was as bewildered as he had been before.

"Uh, no problem," he replied, patting her back awkwardly. He looked over at Amy. "Hey, can I walk you back to the entrance? It's getting dark." Amy rolled her eyes.

"You're so wonderful," Satomi gushed. Connor's cheeks burned.

"Oh, calm down, Satomi," Amy said irritably as she tossed the last of the streamers into the garbage. "I do need to get going though."

"Sure," Connor agreed, beelining toward her.

"Of course you do," Satomi chuckled. "Have a good night, you two. Thanks for helping."

Connor and Amy set off. Once they were out of sight of everyone, they walked a bit closer together, almost brushing.

"Today was great," Amy sighed happily. "Thanks for not fighting with Adam. I know he can be difficult sometimes."

"I would've hated to ruin such a perfect day." They walked back to Amy's apartment and stopped at the staircase.

"How are you getting home?" she asked. "Calling for a ride?"

"Didn't I tell you? I have a car now, so we don't have to worry about having Sheath members around all the time." His stomach still felt cold whenever he pictured the look he'd seen on her face when she saw the other side of him. He never wanted to see it again, so he'd gotten his father to agree to let him have his own car. It had taken a bit of maneuvering, but as a lifelong member of the Sheath, he was born for intrigue.

"That easy, huh?" she asked, doing a bad job of hiding her jealousy. Connor nudged her with his elbow.

"Don't be like that," he said, ruffling her hair. She swatted his hand away, scowling as she fixed it. "You know I'll happily drive you anywhere you want to go." She stuck her tongue out at him.

"I can't help it," she admitted. "But I don't need a car badly enough to ask Arty about it. I don't even have my license yet. Where would I find time for driver's ed?" She sighed. "Good night, Connor."

"Good night, Amy." He watched her go up the stairs and waited until he heard her door close before making his way to his car.

CLASSES STARTED AND SOON, THE WHOLE school was buzzing about the big Homecoming Dance. The dance was in October, but everyone started preparing almost as soon as school started. The whole town got excited for the Homecoming Football Game, a side effect of living in a small town.

Amy wasn't into dances or football, but she loved Spirit Week, and she was supporting the leadership team during it. She didn't have time to run for a leadership position because of her work with the Shield, but every little thing helped on college applications.

Amy walked toward the main hall right as Adam walked into the open area and made eye contact with her. His eyebrows were drawn together, and to her, he looked determined. She smiled and waved.

"Hey, Adam. I was going to catch the bus. Wanna walk

out together? I know you have a car, but maybe you're parked nearby?"

Adam had a weird look on his face that she couldn't quite read, and her stomach churned in response. "I wanted to talk to you," he answered.

"Oh. About what?"

"Well..." He shifted his weight from foot to foot and avoided her eyes. "I've liked you for a while now, and I was wondering if you would go to Homecoming with me?" He looked up at her, his normal bravado gone. He almost looked shy.

This was the Adam only she knew. An uncomfortable lump formed in her throat, and she was grateful the immediate area was empty. "Um... Adam. I'm sorry...uh... I don't really feel the same way. It wouldn't be fair of me to go to Homecoming with you." It was her turn to avoid eye contact.

Adam let out what sounded like a snarl and a sigh combined. Startled, she looked up at him and saw that he was breathing hard, and his hands were shaking. His face was a mottled scarlet and a vein stood out on his forehead.

Amy stepped back.

"No? You're going to say no to *me*?! Me, Adam *Whittaker*?" he hissed, his voice sounded like it was taking all his effort not to yell.

Amy's power responded to her fear, and she tried hard to quell it as her heart pounded.

Adam continued his tirade, making wild and violent hand gestures in the air. "I've been *nicer* to you than anyone else. I thought you were the one person I could be *myself* around. I've been dropping hints for *months*."

Amy balled her hands into fists, trying to keep her power from sparking out. She wasn't sure what she was more frightened of: Adam's violent anger or her potentially deadly response. She stumbled backward, and he advanced on her. "Adam, I thought we were friends," she cried, hating the feeling of tears starting to burn in her eyes. "This isn't like you at all!"

"Friends?" he sneered. "I wanted to be *more* than friends. I could have any girl in this school, but I wanted you." Amy had her arms in front of her, trying to fend him off while simultaneously trying not to blow him and the whole school up. She hadn't felt this close to losing control since she'd first manifested. "But I guess you've been too busy hooking up with Connor." She paused, blinking in confusion.

"W-what?" she stuttered. "What do you mean? I'm not doing anything with Connor." Gulping, she tried to contain the power that roiled instinctively within her.

"Oh, so you've friend-zoned him too?" Adam barked out a laugh. "You disgust me." He made a swipe at her, but she jumped back and ran. She could hear Adam grumbling behind her, but it didn't sound like he was chasing her. She was terrified of what would happen if he did. What would he do to her if he caught her? What would she do to him?

Blinded by the tears she couldn't hold back, she ran out the doors to the backside of the school and straight into someone. Strong hands caught her before she could fall, and in a reflex born from her months of training, she smacked the hands away and put her arms up, fists protecting her jaw. It took her a second to realize who she'd run into.

Connor.

28

Connor

ONNOR HELD HIS HANDS UP, TRYING NOT TO alarm Amy. In his surprise, it took him a moment to realize that she was breathing hard and that tears were running unchecked down her cheeks. *Who did this?* His chest began to burn.

"Amy," he said in what he hoped was a soothing tone. "Amy, are you okay? I could feel you losing control." He could feel her power struggling more than he'd felt since he'd first met her. She straightened a little and began to rub the tears from her eyes and off her cheeks with her sleeves.

"I'm.... I'm fine." Her reply was marred by a barely suppressed sob and a fresh wave of tears running down her face. She covered her eyes with the heels of her hands, seemingly trying to stem the flow. "I'm fine," she repeated shakily.

Connor battled himself to keep his startling anger in check. The need to find the person who did this and crush them took him off guard. He was normally a lot gentler around Amy. Going on instinct, he reached out and pulled her into a tight hug. She half-heartedly tried to push him away, but before he could let her go, she started to sob uncontrollably, her body shaking. Her arms wrapped around him, and she clutched his shirt as she leaned into him and let him support her. He stroked her hair and said nothing as she cried.

They stood there for what felt like forever before she wound down with a hiccup. She finally looked up with red-rimmed eyes. "I'm sorry, Connor," she said with another hiccup.

He laughed, surprised. "Sorry? What for?"

"Um, running into you and then snotting all over your shirt?" A blush spread across her face as she looked at his shirt.

"That's perfectly alright," he replied smoothly, giving in to temptation and running a hand through her hair. It was very soft, reminding him of silk. "What has gotten you so worked up?"

She wiped her eyes again. "You're not gonna to get all macho man upset, are you?" she asked somewhat meekly as she stole a glance at his face. The redness from her crying brought out the startling blue of her eyes. Suddenly, he was grateful for learning to control his emotions at a young age. He would save this anger for whoever did this.

"Me, macho? Never," he said with a grin. "I'm far too sophisticated for such things." He flipped his hair with exaggerated haughtiness in an attempt to make her laugh. She stepped out of his arms without responding and looked at the ground. He felt oddly bereft without her but didn't reach out.

"It's Adam," she said. Connor felt his insides turn to ice, and the Sword roared again for blood. He breathed in deeply through his nose before responding.

"Adam?"

"Yeah. He—he told me he liked me, and he asked me to Homecoming. I told him no and that I didn't feel the same. I promise I was nice about it," she said desperately. She stepped toward Connor, seemingly trying to convince him she'd done nothing wrong. "But h-he didn't take it well. He was yelling at me. And the Shield—it took everything in me to not let it vaporize him. I don't know what was scarier," she cried, the tears starting up again. She put her face into her hands and hunched over. "Me or him."

The ice inside him slowly melted and was replaced by a deep, gut-burning sense of rage. He pulled her into his arms again, tucking her head under his chin. "Amy, you could never be scary. You're the sweetest person I know. Adam never deserved your friendship. He's a worthless, slimy bug."

He had to fight the urge to wipe the tears from her eyes when she peeked up at him before she put her head back down, leaning into him. Feeling her in his arms was foreign, but he found that it warmed a part of him he hadn't known existed, and more importantly, it kept his power from exploding outwards.

"You're right," she said, the tears clearing up from her voice. "He isn't worth it. He wasn't really my friend after all." The hurt in her voice caused a sensation in his chest that he wasn't sure how to identify, something akin to a stab. "Thank you, Connor. You're a friend who's worth it." She moved some hair out of his eyes, then looked away. With a start, she pulled away from him. "Crap, I need to go catch my bus. See you later, okay?" she called as she sprinted away as fast as she could. He watched her go, not trusting himself to speak further.

He walked robotically into the school. He was going to find Adam because they were going to have a little talk. He looked into the wing where he assumed Amy had come from and saw that Adam was still there. The pathetic excuse for a boy was furiously typing away at his phone—the nerve. *Probably texting people a made up story to protect his fragile ego.* The camera nearby made a weird noise as his power fried it. The Sheath did not operate in the open after all and in this moment, Connor was all Sheath.

Approaching silently, Connor backhanded the phone out of Adam's hands. Adam looked up with surprise as Connor grabbed the front of his shirt and slammed him into a wall. The Sword flared, excitedly waiting to draw blood.

Adam struggled. Despite his stocky build, he was nothing compared to Connor's rage. Upon apparently determining he was outmatched, he stopped and sneered into Connor's face. "So, she sent you after me, huh? I knew she was hooking up with you." Connor pulled Adam back and slammed him into the wall again. The stone started cracking, and Adam's eyes went wide. He kept his mouth shut as he gaped at Connor.

"Now you listen to me, you disgusting, sorry excuse for a man," Connor snarled, putting his face right up to Adam's. "If I find you speaking ill of Amy or if you come anywhere near her again, I will put your head through this wall and make sure that you do not get back up. Do. You. Understand?" he growled and lifted Adam even higher. It disgusted him how much he sounded like his father, but he couldn't control the burning rage, and the Sword certainly wasn't helping things any.

Adam, pathetic as he was, nodded quickly, stammering his understanding. Connor backhanded him, which drew a bit of blood from his lip. A knot immediately formed in Connor's stomach at the sight. *I am acting too much like father, but it is necessary.* The Sword rejoiced. Adam gasped and tried to cover his face. Connor dropped him and stepped back. Adam sat on the floor, his eyes wide with fear.

Without a second glance, Connor walked away and left him there, stepping on Adam's phone on his way out. He smiled as the screen crunched under his heel.

He walked out of the school and to his car, unconsciously driving to Amy's apartment, studies be damned. He arrived well before she did and played on his phone for about twenty minutes before he saw Amy walk up. She was looking down as she walked with her shoulders hunched, and he could tell that she had been crying again. He suddenly wished that he'd at least broken one of Adam's bones. Quickly squashing his more violent side, he exited the car.

"Amy!" he called, waving at her. She looked up, startled, and then smiled sadly at him.

"Hey, Connor, what're you doing here?" Her voice was hoarse.

"I thought I'd come by to check on you. I apologize, I should have offered you a ride home."

"I'm not gonna be very good company," Amy said as she walked past him, climbing the stairs to her apartment unit. Connor followed behind her.

"That's alright." They reached her apartment, and she unlocked the door, letting him in. She threw her stuff to the ground and walked over to the couch, flopped onto it, and buried her head into a pillow. Connor sat on the floor beside her head.

"I am the stupidest person on the face of the planet," she moaned into a pillow, curling into a ball. He rubbed her back soothingly. Touching her felt natural and normal now. The dam had been broken, and he couldn't seem to help himself.

"Hey, no you're not." He hoped desperately that he sounded reassuring.

"I am. Everyone said he was a jerk, but I didn't listen. I believed the side of him he showed me was the real him. I really am naïve."

"I can't deny that you're a bit naïve," Connor said. Amy lifted her head slightly to glare at him. "But it's endearing. You see the good in everyone, which makes you an amazing friend. Don't let one bad apple spoil everything for you."

She buried her head in the pillow and went silent. He continued rubbing her back, letting her lie there. After a time, Arty unlocked the front door. Amy didn't move, so Connor didn't either.

"I'm home," Arty called from the entryway.

"We're in the living room," Connor replied after waiting to see if Amy would say anything. Arty stopped when he saw Amy lying on the couch. He was so concerned that he didn't even seem to notice Connor snatching his hand away from her back, much to Connor's relief.

"What's wrong?" he asked, immediately slipping into pseudo-dad mode. Connor looked at Amy, who didn't look up or speak.

"Adam." Connor said simply. Amy curled into an even tighter ball at the mention of his name, and Arty went and sat by her feet. With a start, Connor realized he didn't look so goofy anymore. His stomach twisted as he imagined that look being directed at him if he ever learned the truth.

"Amy, what happened? What did Adam do?" Arty asked gently.

"Do you want me to call Satomi so you only have to tell the story once if you're ready to talk?" Connor asked, trying to be helpful.

"Or do you want to just talk to me? Connor can go home if you want," Arty interjected. Connor flinched at his tone.

"Honestly, I'd rather tell you and Satomi at the same time, I don't wanna repeat myself a bunch. And I want Connor to stay." Arty looked up at Connor and nodded. Amy took out her phone and called Satomi.

"Hullo," Satomi answered on the second ring, sounding chipper. "What's up, Ames?" Amy let out a sob. "Ames, what happened?" Satomi asked softly.

Breaking into a fresh wave of tears, she told them the whole story, leaving out the parts about the Shield. When she was done, Connor was worried that Arty was going to have a stroke, and Satomi was swearing up a storm. Through the maelstrom, Connor stayed close to Amy and remained silent. After all, he'd already taken care of things on his end.

"I'm calling his parents," Arty said angrily, standing.

Amy grabbed at his shirt. "Please don't," she begged. "He'll make my life hell."

"I don't think he will," Connor said, and Amy shot him a glare.

"Connor, what did you do?" Her tone was demanding, but her red-rimmed eyes took away the edge.

"Nothing," he said lightly. "I don't think he'll do anything in retaliation is all." He barely suppressed a vicious grin. *He won't retaliate if he knows what's good for him.*

Arty looked at him, understanding flashing in his eyes. "I knew I liked you." Connor stopped suppressing the grin.

"You can't let him get away with something so awful!" Satomi yelled from the phone.

"Well, no," Amy conceded. Connor was worried that she was going to cry again, so he moved to sit directly beside her instead of on the ground. Without hesitation, she rested her head against him, and he felt his pulse kick up. *Odd.* "Okay, Arty," she said after a moment. Connor thought Arty looked like he was going to have a stroke as he looked at where Amy's head rested.

"Attagirl!" Satomi cheered. Her parents could be heard in the background. "I've got to get off the phone, but I'll see you tomorrow, okay?"

"Good night, Satomi."

"Night, Ames." Amy hung up, and Arty stomped out of the room and was immediately on the line with Adam's parents, telling them what had happened.

"There," Arty said, satisfied, when he came back just a few minutes later. "Maybe that will teach the spoiled little monster a lesson." Connor didn't think much would happen to the "Whittaker Prince" but didn't say anything. "Do you want anything to eat?" he asked Amy, concern replacing the anger on his face.

"I'm not hungry," she mumbled. Arty looked at them and sighed.

"I'm going to go do some work stuff in my room. Let me know when you get hungry."

"Okay."

Arty left, and it was just Amy and Connor in the room.

"How's the Shield?" Connor asked quietly once he heard Arty's bedroom door close.

"It keeps trying to make a bubble around me," she answered, sniffling. "What did you do to Adam?"

"Who says I did anything?" She looked pointedly at him. "I told him, *politely*, not to do anything stupid."

"You assaulted him, didn't you?"

He shrugged. "Define assault."

Amy groaned and thumped her forehead against his shoulder.

"What am I going to do with you?" she asked, grinning up at him. "You can't go assaulting people all willy-nilly." She smacked him, hard, on the arm.

"You just assaulted me!"

Amy rolled her eyes, then stood and stretched. "I'm going to work on homework. Did you bring yours?"

"I have my backpack in my car. I'll go and get it."

"Perfect."

CONNOR WENT HOME THAT EVENING FEELING warmth both in his stomach from the pizza they had ordered and, in his chest, though he wasn't sure what that was from. As he drove home, his mood soured. *What am I doing? She's my enemy, my family's enemy. Why did I defend her? I just... I wasn't thinking. I should have teamed up with Adam or something, anything! Hopefully Father never gets wind. I can't seem to help myself when she's around.*

He made it to his room, flopping on his bed. He covered his eyes with an arm and groaned. *What is wrong with me?* Amy's eyes flashed through his mind, capturing his attention like they always did, and that warmth came flooding back into his chest. He froze, trying to make sense of the strange feeling.

My caring about her is only an act... right? He moaned and ran his hands up his face and through his hair. *This is so confusing.* As he thought more about Amy, his heart beat harder, and his face heated. Groaning, he rolled onto his stomach and covered his head with his pillow.

Why did she have to be the Shield host?

29

Amy

AT LUNCH, CONNOR, AMY, AND SATOMI SAT together, more subdued than usual. Amy was barely picking at her food while Satomi and Connor watched her with worry etched on their faces. Satomi was barely even making a mess today. About halfway through lunch, Amy heard Adam's booming voice coming toward them, and her stomach dropped as she looked down.

C'mon Adam. Not here, not now.

"Hey Amy," he thundered, slamming his hands down on the lunch table with a loud smack. She jumped, her eyes shooting up to his red face. "You can't avoid me anymore. You got me in a lot of trouble last night. Do you even know who I am?" Connor started to rise, but Amy allowed her power to surge within her as a warning. He froze, and his eyes shot to her as she stood. *How dare he try to embarrass me like this?* Her power flowed throughout her body and her fear vanished. *I don't deserve this.*

"I know exactly who you are," she said firmly and loudly. Her eyes flickered gold for a brief second as her voice carried across the room. The cafeteria went silent as everyone turned and watched. She circled the table until she was within a few feet of Adam, staring at him eye to eye. "You're a pathetic, spoiled brat who can't handle not getting his way. I rejected you, and like the child you are, you tried to *attack* me. I don't give a damn that you're a 'Whittaker.' Your hard-working ancestors would be ashamed of you. If you *ever* try to lay hands on me again, I'll make sure you regret it."

The silence that hung in the air after her statement was deafening.

Adam stared at her, his face turning a more vibrant shade of red, and his fists clenched. The entire lunchroom was watching silently. Amy wasn't sure if they were surprised to hear her raise her voice or surprised to see someone stand up to Adam.

Adam's breathing became almost labored with obvious rage. Suddenly, he swung a fist at her face. Satomi gasped, but Amy saw him telegraph what he was planning. She dodged, stepping out of the way. A vein on Adam's face started to pulse, but his eyes looked more sad than angry as they shimmered with tears. *Geez, stop making your tantrum my problem.* As Adam pulled a fist back again, two teachers were there, pulling him back and dragging him out of the lunchroom as people gasped. He seemed to deflate as he looked back at Amy.

Ms. Timmings, an English teacher, came up to Amy as she went to sit back down. "Are you okay, Amy?" she asked. "Do you need the nurse or anything?"

"I'm okay, he didn't get me. Am I in trouble?"

"No, we saw what happened. We'll have to call your guardian to inform them, but you're not in any trouble."

Gradually, other students started talking excitedly and pointing in their direction.

"I feel a little better," Amy said happily after Ms. Timmings left. Connor smirked.

Satomi looked like she was either going to faint or explode. "You... you..." she spluttered and pointed limply at Amy.

Amy raised an eyebrow. "I what?"

"You... how..." She shook her head. "That was the most awesome thing I have ever seen in my entire life!" Her arms gesticulated wildly.

"If you say so," Amy said. Despite herself, she grinned. "It was pretty fun."

"How did you do that though? He's a behemoth."

Amy squirmed. "I've been working out, and Arty has had me taking some self-defense lessons. You have to watch what their bodies are doing."

"And you didn't tell me?" Satomi asked. A pit formed in Amy's stomach. *More lies.*

"I didn't think it was that exciting," she replied with a shrug. "But I'm sorry I didn't mention it. It slipped my mind."

Satomi patted her arm. "It's okay. It's not a huge thing or anything. It's not like you were hiding it." Amy's body was heavy with the lies.

The bell rang, and Satomi shot up, dumped her garbage in a nearby trash can, and put away her tray at the speed of light. "See you in art!" she shouted. Amy sighed, literally saved by the bell.

Connor patted her shoulder. "That didn't look fun." She shook her head. "If it's any consolation, you putting Adam in his place was the most amazing thing I have ever seen. I'll be replaying that in my head forever."

Amy laughed and stood as Connor did. She threw her arms around Connor's middle and hugged him, pressing her face against his chest. "Let them talk," she said in a muffled voice. He had his arms up in surprise but wrapped them around her soon enough.

"My people will talk as well," he whispered. She froze. "Don't worry. They want me close to you. This is a good thing." She pulled away and looked up at him.

"If you say so."

30

Amy

AMY'S SEVENTEENTH BIRTHDAY PASSED WITH little fanfare, just Connor and Satomi at her apartment eating pizza and watching movies. It took a few weeks, but the school stopped gossiping about Amy and Adam. He walked around with a permanent scowl on his face, his normal charming smile gone.

When Homecoming arrived, Amy went over to Satomi's house and helped her get ready, and they took pictures together, as was their tradition. She left before Satomi's date, Eric, got there, making sure to give her an extra big hug while extracting a promise from Satomi to tell her everything the next day at school and to take a ton of pictures.

She went back home and straight to the couch, unsure of what to do with herself. Arty had left for a weekend work conference, leaving behind money for food. After mulling it over, she changed into her comfiest, rattiest pajamas, put on her old, pink bunny slippers, and put her hair into pigtail braids like she was a kid again, trying to pretend that she didn't have responsibilities anymore. If she was going to be home alone, she was going to have a "me-day" for herself and eat pizza and ice cream while watching sappy movies and having a good cry. She deserved it.

After finding nothing streaming, she went through Arty's old DVDs, pulling out the first movie she wanted to watch right as the doorbell rang. Jumping slightly, she walked over to gaze out the peephole. Her face burned as she yanked her eye away and attempted to hide herself from view. Connor was outside, and she was *not* dressed for company. She glanced down frantically at herself, wringing her hands.

God, what am I supposed to do?

Forcing herself to breathe deeply, she realized that Connor had probably sensed her freak out via the Sword, which was almost as mortifying as opening that door would be. *Oh, forget it.* She gritted her teeth and opened the door. "Hey, Connor," she said with forced enthusiasm. "What's up?"

"I thought you might like some company since you weren't going to the dance," he said, glossing over whatever he may have sensed. He looked anything but ratty in his normal, tailored ensemble. Amy wished for the millionth time that her powers allowed her to be sucked into the ground.

"Aren't you going? You had to have had at least a dozen girls ask." Amy opened the door wider and waved him in.

Connor grinned as he entered. "Only three or four and one very charming gentleman. I turned them all down, however. I don't usually go to school events." His eyes darted up and down her outfit. Now she wanted the ground-swallowing powers for a million and one times.

"I was just gonna watch some movies and order pizza." *Why did he have to be here now, of all times? Couldn't he have at least called first? Or texted? Sent a carrier pigeon? Something—anything?!*

"Would you like me to go?" he asked mildly. Obviously, he wasn't blind to her scarlet face. She sighed.

"Since you're already here and you've seen me in all my glory, you might as well stay." She stomped over to the couch. "But you have to put in the movie."

"Such ancient technology." He picked up the DVD case that Amy had left on top of it, making a face as he read the title. "*Titanic?*"

"I wanted a good cry," Amy said. "I had planned on binge-eating pizza and ice cream while watching sappy movies all night."

He put down the movie and looked at her, a strange emotion flitting across his face. Amy felt her stomach clench at whatever it was. "Amy, did you have feelings for Adam? You sound like you went through a breakup."

She stared at him, disbelief filling her. "Why does everyone think that?" she exploded. "No, I didn't have a thing for him. I legitimately thought he was one of my best friends, so much so that I overlooked what a jackass he was. If I'm acting like I broke up with someone it's because I *did*. I went through a friend breakup, and it hurts, okay?" Amy couldn't help the tears that sprang up, and she dashed them away angrily. "Sorry I'm not over it yet." She scrubbed at her eyes again. "But no, I didn't have a crush on Adam."

She glared at him. "Why? You jealous?" Her cheeks burned at the impulsive question and butterflies fluttered in her stomach. Why had she said *that* of all things? Where were ground-swallowing powers when you needed them?

He looked at her a moment longer, not answering, his face blank. He put the DVD in and then looked back at her. Amy squirmed. She was about to take back her question when Connor replied. "What if I was?" he asked inscrutably.

Her heart galloped and her mouth went dry. The DVD's menu song started playing, but she couldn't look away from Connor's piercing gaze. She wasn't sure whether she had somehow unknowingly ingested an entire swarm of butterflies or if she was about to suddenly be sick.

"I don't know," she whispered.

"This is an incredibly inappropriate time to say this..." he began but trailed off. Amy was pretty sure she was going to throw up on him as her knees began to tremble. Was he going to say that he liked her like Adam had? And why did that make her feel all warm and tingly? *Oh God, do I like, like him?* Connor had stopped talking. He looked away with a frown.

Why couldn't she control her breathing?

As she looked at him, a beautiful and horrible realization dawned on her. All the time they spent together, their shared fate, his green eyes, his rare smiles—everything flashed through her mind in a second. Like how she wanted to see him every single day and how she missed him when he was gone, no matter how much she denied it. The realization that their time was short grounded her, and she calmed herself as she saw things clearly for the first time.

"Connor," she said, standing up and walking toward him. She reached up and placed a hand on his cheek, forcing him to look at her. He looked at her questioningly.

"Forget it," he said with a warm smile, placing his hand on hers. "Let's watch your movie and binge your... junk food." He faked a shudder.

She couldn't speak. She opened her mouth, but no sound came out. What she needed to convey needed to be conveyed *now*, with or without words. The truth of it resonated in her soul. Leaning close to him, she paused, her lips an inch from his. His sharp intake of breath was the only sound before he placed a hand on the back of her head and tilted it back. He closed the gap between them and kissed her softly.

She was pretty sure that fireworks had started going off inside the apartment. Actually, with their powers, that was a real possibility. Wrapping her arms around his neck, she pulled him closer and lost herself in the warmth of the moment that felt like it lasted forever.

"So, I guess you were jealous," Amy said, blurting the first thing that popped into her head as they parted.

Connor laughed. "I guess I was." He kissed her again, more firmly this time, twining his fingers in her hair. She sighed as her lips parted.

BOOM.

The spirits within them met and sent them flying backward.

Why could she see the ceiling?

Amy's eyes fluttered open. She sat up, rubbing her head. Belatedly, she realized the pounding she heard wasn't in her head but was the sound of frantic knocking on her front door. She leapt up. Trying to appear as calm as possible, she opened the door to a handful of her neighbors.

"What was that noise, dear? Is everything okay?" the elderly Mrs. Vasquez from next door asked. She was evidently going to be the spokesperson for the group.

"I am so, so sorry, Mrs. Vasquez," Amy said. The elderly woman grimaced. "I was moving a heavy mirror and dropped it. The sound startled me too. But don't worry, the mirror didn't break, I didn't get hurt, and I won't touch it again until Arty gets home." She looked at the small crowd with pleading eyes. "I know it was dumb."

"There, there," Mrs. Vasquez said, patting her shoulder affectionately. "We're glad you're okay." There was a murmur of agreement from around her. "Don't try to do such dangerous things on your own anymore." Her voice took on the scolding tone Amy had heard her use on her grandkids before.

"I promise," Amy replied. "Thank you all for understanding and for checking in on me." The crowd dispersed, and she shut the door, rushing toward Connor, who was sitting up with a groan.

"That was a hell of a kiss," he said, winking. She rolled her eyes.

"We probably should have known. We can control them when we touch, but anything more and they take over."

"Anything *more*?" He winked again, and she slapped his arm. "I'm sorry, but you were wide open for that one."

"Oh, grow up," she said, resuming her seat on the couch. She looked around and was pleased to find that there was no damage to anything but her pride.

"We should probably talk though," he said.

"What do we need to talk about?" she asked, raising an eyebrow. "I like you, you like me. We're going to kill each other at some point. It all seems rather cut and dry, really. We don't have a lot of time on this earth, so let's make the most of it. Let's be together."

Connor stared. "Together?" he choked.

"Together," she said. "Best friends."

"Just friends?"

"Connor," she said, amused. "We are so much more than friends."

"We are?" He prodded, seemingly unable to say what he was hinting at. Fortunately for him, Amy wasn't nearly as emotionally repressed as he was.

"Connor, we're practically dating already, let's cut the crap. Do you want to date or not?"

He picked her up in a fierce hug and spun her around before kissing her with all the emotions he couldn't say, his mouth firmly closed. "Traditionally, shouldn't I be the one asking you?" he asked. She smacked his chest, and he laughed. "But yes, Amy Sanders, I want to date you."

"So formal," she teased, then wiggled out of his arms to go back to the couch where she patted the seat beside her. "Come and watch the movie with me." She picked up the remote and pressed play. Connor resumed his seat, placing an arm around her. She snuggled close to him, wrapping her arms around his middle and resting her head on his chest with a contented sigh. This felt like where she belonged.

When she'd learned she was the Shield's host, she'd felt the truth in the core of her being. This felt much the same.

They watched the movie, snuggling and kissing throughout. Then they watched another. And another.

"Wow, time really got away from me," Connor said, checking his cell phone.

"You should probably get going before your family gets upset," Amy said.

"Where is Arty?"

"Did you only just now realize he isn't here?" She laughed.

"I was otherwise occupied."

"He's gone overnight for work."

"You're staying here alone?" he asked, concerned. She cocked an eyebrow.

"Connor, I am more dangerous than almost anyone else in the world." She created a ball of energy in her hand to prove her point. "I'm pretty sure I can handle a night alone in Whittaker Hills."

"But still. Isn't it scary to sleep here all alone?"

Amy shrugged. "Not really. I've done it before. I turn on some quiet music so I don't get weirded out by any random noises I hear." She grabbed his arm and shoved him toward the door. "Go home."

"Fine, fine." Connor put his shoes on. "So..." He stood. "Is this dating thing public knowledge?"

Amy thought about it. "Will that cause an issue within the Sheath?"

Connor started. "I'm not sure," he replied. "They wanted me to get close to the Shield's host. Can't get much closer than this." He shrugged. "I can spin it the right way." He stooped to drop a kiss on her forehead. "Good night, Amy."

He left and she closed the door. She leapt up, spun in the air, and dropped backward onto a golden bubble to float dreamily down to the ground, covering her flushed face with her hands. Her first-ever boyfriend *and* her first kiss on the same night? She couldn't wait to tell Satomi.

31

Amy

THE NEXT DAY, AMY CLOSED AND LOCKED HER apartment door, her mind still reeling from the previous night. She played the memories over and over again, her heart beating a bit harder than usual.

Connor was waiting at the foot of the stairs. With a happy little squeal, Amy threw herself into his arms. He caught her and squeezed her gently before bending down and kissing her. She hadn't been imagining it last night—kissing Connor was heaven. His lips were warm and soft, and she felt safe in his arms, ironic given how they met and what their fate was. She sighed when they broke apart and looked up at him with a smile.

"I was almost worried last night was a dream," she said, grinning up at him. He stood several inches above her, so her chin rested on his sternum.

"Are you saying I'm the man of your dreams?" he joked. She laughed.

"What are you doing here so early?" she asked.

"I thought I'd drive my girlfriend to school." Amy stared at him.

"But what about the Sheath?" She swore she saw his eyes darken at the mention of them, but it quickly passed.

"They think this is the perfect setup. Can't get much closer than this." He kissed her forehead.

"I won't complain if it means I get to see you more. Plus, I hate the bus."

Holding hands, they made their way to Connor's car, a silver Mercedes. Amy did her best not to stare, but it was hard. Luxury cars were pretty rare in Whittaker Hills. Cars weren't really her thing, but she could tell it was expensive. He led her to the passenger door, opening it for her.

"Wait, you actually know how to open car doors?" she teased while getting in. The car smelled new and, even though she was morally opposed to leather, she couldn't help noticing that the interior of this car was pristine and beautiful. Everything was black or silver and shone. Arty's car was generally a bit cluttered and would never be called *pristine*.

Connor opened his door and got in, putting on his seatbelt. Amy couldn't help but notice how well dressed he was. Idly, she wondered again if he had everything tailored or custom-made. He looked over at her. "Is this okay? I've never, you know... had a girlfriend before." She stared at him for a beat, unaccustomed to him sounding unsure in any setting. She reached out and squeezed his hand.

"Of course! I'm happy to see you any time, and I'm never going to say no to not having to ride the bus," she said. "I've never had a boyfriend before, so we can bumble along together. This isn't a bother for you, is it?" she asked shyly, looking up at him from under her lashes. "Picking me up?"

"Of course it isn't. It gets me out of the house sooner, and I don't have to spend as much time with Peter and Quinton."

"Are they really not your friends at all?"

Connor snorted as he pulled out into the street. "I wouldn't call appointed friends, actual friends."

"You have Satomi and me now." The ghost of a half-smile flashed across his face as they continued on their way to school. It felt like only a minute before they were there.

When Connor pulled into a parking space, he turned to look at Amy and said, "Stay," in a firm voice.

"I'm not a dog."

"Stay for a second," he said as he got out of the car. Amy watched him through the windows as he walked around the car to her side and opened her door. He held out his hand to help her out of the car. Her cheeks heated as she took it.

"You know, I can open doors on my own."

He smiled at her, keeping her hand in his as they walked toward the school entrance. "I am well aware. Humor me." She laced her fingers through his. He was polished, perhaps he couldn't help himself.

They held hands through the halls, which seemed to spark a quiet uproar. People were probably surprised that Connor, the handsome newer kid, was dating Amy Sanders, the plain girl who'd rejected Adam. She wasn't sure if people actually thought she was plain, but she assumed so when compared with Connor or Adam.

They stopped when they heard a loud squeal, and before either of them could react, Satomi threw herself at them, words tumbling out of her mouth in an incomprehensible jumble, her form a blur of neon. Amy barely managed to keep her hand in Connor's as she was jolted to the side.

"You— and YOU—and *TOGETHER*?!" she finally finished, breathless.

"It happened last night," Amy said. Satomi squealed again and hugged Amy so hard around the neck that she could barely breathe.

Satomi released her and then danced around, clapping, before doing the same to Connor. He awkwardly patted her back while looking at Amy beseechingly. She shrugged. "I can't really do anything about her," she said apologetically.

Satomi let go of Connor and turned to Amy with shining eyes. "My ship has sailed!" she squealed, spinning again. Amy couldn't help but laugh.

"Satomi, where'd you go?" Amy turned when she heard her friend's name called, but not before catching her blush. Eric, Satomi's Homecoming date, was walking toward them. Amy didn't miss the telltale signs of puppy love all over his face—the dark skin of his cheeks was tinted red too. His plain clothes and tall build were a delightful contrast to Satomi's neon, petite one.

"Hi, Amy," he said as he wrapped an arm around Satomi's waist and pulled her close. Satomi's blush spread.

"We decided that one date wasn't enough," Satomi said, looking shyly up at Amy.

"Aw, that's so great!" Amy beamed.

"Satomi has told me a lot about you, and you, Connor," Eric said, smiling up at Connor and holding his hand out. Connor had stiffened, but his charming smile turned on immediately as he shook Eric's hand.

"A pleasure to meet you," he murmured. Eric shook out his hand once Connor let it go. Before anyone could speak, the first bell rang.

"See you at lunch," Eric said, then he dropped a kiss on Satomi's cheek. "It was nice meeting you. Well, I guess talking to you since we've sort of met before in classes," he said, waving to Amy. "Connor," he said with a nod. The second he was out of earshot in the crowd, Amy hugged Satomi tightly.

"I can't believe we got our first boyfriends on the same night," she said happily, letting her go.

Satomi smiled, her eyes lighting up. "I said he can sit with us at lunch, I hope that's okay."

"Of course it is, right, Connor?" Amy asked. She hadn't missed the hand-crushing moment.

Connor shrugged. "Of course," he said with forced warmth. "We had better get going if we don't want to be late," he said, reaching for Amy's hand. "We'll see you at lunch, Satomi."

"Bye!" Amy called back as Connor pulled her away. "What was that about?"

Connor didn't respond right away, seemingly lost in thought. "I don't know. I got so used to it being us three, I guess I wasn't ready for someone new," he admitted.

Amy wrapped her arms around his arm, hugging him warmly. "Don't worry, Eric is a good guy. We don't talk much, but he's always been really nice to everyone. He's in the chess club and plays tennis, so he's a brainy jock. I like him."

"I'll give him a chance."

32

Amy

"Today has been so awk-weird," Amy commented at lunch. They were at their normal lunch table. Amy sat between Satomi and Connor and thought maybe it would be best if Connor didn't sit close to Eric, as he didn't seem very comfortable yet.

"Everyone's just jealous of how adorable you two are," Satomi gushed happily, chowing down on her lunch with gusto. "He's also the first boyfriend you've ever had, and it's such a small town that everyone knows."

Amy slammed her head onto the table. "I hate being gawked at," she moaned. "Why aren't they staring at you and Eric?" she demanded, gesturing to the two of them. While Satomi ate with zeal, Eric cut calmly into his meal with a fork and knife.

"Probably because I didn't publicly turn down the

'Whittaker Prince,'" Satomi said nonchalantly, wiping at some sauce on her face.

"Wait, you actually did that?" Eric exclaimed, his gaze snapping up to Amy's face. "I was absent that day, but I heard about it."

She flushed. "He didn't take no very well." she explained, looking down.

"You are so freaking cool," he said finally. "I hate that guy, he's such a jerk." Connor's stiff shoulders loosened slightly.

"She is pretty cool," he agreed, patting his mouth elegantly with a napkin. "I enjoyed the moment immensely. I suppose I should thank the clod though. If he hadn't been such a jerk, this," he said gesturing between himself and Amy, "might not have happened as soon."

"Connor was *super* jealous of Adam," Satomi explained to Eric in a loud, exaggerated whisper.

"I was *not*," he snapped, but his cheeks pinkened. "I merely thought he was a jerk, and I was right is all." He went back to eating, looking at no one.

"It's okay, Connor, though I was never interested in him." Amy consoled him with a hand on his shoulder. He glanced sideways at her but didn't reply, clearly still trying to get his cheeks to cool. She grinned and went back to eating.

A MY HOISTED HER BACKPACK ONTO HER SHOUL-der, grunting slightly under its weight. Walking quickly, she dodged bodies and clumps of people to get out to the front of the school where the parking lot was. The lack of lockers at the school made her backpack heavy some days. She tried to think of it as extra Shield training.

She found Connor's car, which stood out even to her unknowledgeable gaze. Not seeing Connor around, she dug her phone out of her pocket to text him. Before she could start the text, her phone was yanked out of her hands. Startled, she looked up and saw Adam holding it and glaring at her. His blue eyes looked darker than normal, and his gaze seemed menacing.

"You and Connor, huh?" he sneered, twirling the phone precariously in his hand. Amy felt her anger surge, and her power began to awaken, searing a burning path through her body. She clenched her fist but held still, worried about her phone. And not blowing up Adam.

"Give me back my phone, Adam," she said evenly as her stance automatically widened. The slumbering spirit within her slowly started to stir upon feeling the activation of her powers. The spirit's approval flashed through her mind at her form before slipping back into sleep.

Adam tossed her phone in the air, catching it and then smirking at her. "Nah, I want to have a little chat. First, you turned *me* down and made me the laughingstock of the whole school. Now you're rubbing salt in the wound by going out with pretty boy *Connor*," he almost spat the name. He caught the phone again. "Did you really think I was gonna let that fly?"

Amy rolled her eyes, unable to help herself. "You did that on your own, it isn't my fault that you're a spoiled brat who can't stand to hear the word 'no.'" Adam tossed the phone into the air again. It didn't come back down. He looked up behind him to where Connor's green eyes bore down on him with a fiery intensity that gave Amy pause.

She thought she felt the air around them get a bit chillier as the crackling of power filled her ears. Impressive that she could barely sense it. And concerning.

Adam couldn't feel what Amy felt, but even he could tell something was different. Connor was stone-still, staring at Adam, who appeared unable to break eye contact. Amy was aware that the whole parking lot had gone quiet as everyone watched.

Oh no, this is bad.

"What," Connor began in a voice of steel, "do you think you're doing?" He held the phone where he had caught it, his eyes not leaving Adam's.

Adam's face colored. He could no doubt feel all eyes on him. "I'm having a word with your 'girlfriend' here," he jeered. "She was mine before she was with you." He had made a grave error the second he mentioned her, and she had already started to move. She smoothly caught Connor's arm by the wrist right before his fist made contact, stopping it within an inch of Adam's face. His blackening gaze shot to her, and she held it, gripping his wrist tightly, ignoring the pain of her power's reaction. Adam had frozen, eyes wide.

"He isn't worth it, Connor," she said calmly, trying to use her eyes to tell him they couldn't use their powers publicly while simultaneously trying to wrestle her own down. Every instinct screamed at her to jump back and gather her power to fight, but she held her ground, refusing even to blink. Beads of cold sweat formed on her forehead.

After what felt like forever, but was probably only a few seconds, Connor blinked and the darkness in his eyes vanished. Amy slowly let go of his wrist while Adam stumbled backward as if being released by an invisible force.

"You're both freaks!" he yelled while fleeing, his pride clearly forgotten.

Connor stared down at Amy, his expression turning both contrite and stubborn. "You should have let me hit him," he grumbled, stomping past her to open her door. "Get in before I run after him and finish what he started."

Amy didn't move. "You are out of control, and you need to calm down before someone gets hurt." Her voice was unwavering, though quiet enough not to carry. He sighed, and his shoulders slumped slightly.

"It'll be easier if we leave," he countered.

"If I get in and you immediately run after him, I'm gonna key your car," she warned. She hoped it was a good enough threat—guys usually liked their cars. For a moment, he looked horrified. Then, unexpectedly, he threw his head back and laughed. She felt the tension and power in the air disperse and she herself relaxed, smiling sheepishly. "What's so funny?"

"Key my car?" he chuckled, running a hand through his hair and looking at her with a grin. "That's your big threat?"

"Well yeah... it's a really nice car," she mumbled.

He walked over to her and put a finger under her chin, lifting her head to look at him. "You're ridiculous in the best way," he said, leaning down to briefly kiss her. She blinked as he released her and made his way to the driver's side. "You can close your own door for that."

"You are the weirdest person I've ever met," she groaned, then got in and closed the door behind her. She could already hear the excited buzz of people talking as it shut. Connor got in and looked over at her, his face serious.

"Hey, I am sorry about that," he said, putting his hand on her balled-up one. He looked repentant. "I shouldn't have lost my temper. When I saw him over here, it took all my might not to obliterate him."

Amy put her other hand on top of his and squeezed it. "It's okay, he has that effect on me as well." Connor grinned. He pulled his hand back and took her phone out of his pocket to hand to her. She wasn't sure when he'd managed to stash it out of harm's way, but she'd been otherwise occupied. "Thanks for saving my phone, though. I don't have any upgrades available right now, so I'm not sure what I'd have done if he'd broken it."

Connor smiled as he started the car and backed out into the line of traffic leaving the school. "I could have bought you a new one," he half-joked, stopping to let a blue truck into the line.

Amy smacked his arm. "Rich boy." She laughed and finally felt the Shield settle in her mind. It wasn't quite asleep, but it wasn't all the way awake either.

"I am," he admitted jovially. "Usually girls go for that." He glanced at her.

"If I wanted a rich boy, I could have dated that pinhead." His knuckles went white briefly as he clutched his steering wheel.

"Yuck."

"Yuck is right." She giggled again. "Want to go to the park? I'll let Arty know I won't be home right away."

"Sure, I could use a jog." Amy blanched. "What?" he asked, perplexed.

"If we're going to work out, then we have to stop at my place so I can change." No way was she jogging in jeans and a sweatshirt with no sports bra.

C ONNOR PARKED AT AMY'S BUILDING. "WAIT HERE. I'll be right back," she said brightly as she ran out of the car and up the stairs.

Amy rushed to her room and dressed as fast as she could before running back out. "I'm back!" she said happily as she opened the door. He stared at her.

"You look lovely," he said after jerking his eyes up to hers before starting the car as she buckled her seat belt.

She scoffed. "You've seen me in workout clothes before." Amy took over the radio to annoy him with pop music.

They pulled into the parking lot and got out, taking time to stretch at the nearest trailhead after doing a quick warm-up.

"Think you can keep up with me?" Connor teased.

"Psh, long legs aren't everything," she retorted, standing up and bending backward to stretch out her lower back. "I've trained with Arty, and he's ninety percent leg." He let out a loud bark of laughter.

"You're not wrong. Ready to go?"

"Yep!" she yelled, already launching herself down the trail.

"That's cheating!" Connor yelled as he chased after her. Amy kept her lead, certain he was letting her win, but trying her best anyway. She knew this park better than anyone and took every shortcut she could think of to lose him. Of course, she didn't.

Finally, she burst into the familiar clearing they trained in so often. "I win!" she shouted, fist pumping in the air. He ran in and scooped her up bridal style. She yelped and grabbed onto his neck with a surprised shout as he spun her around and plopped her onto the ground. She didn't release him, and he tumbled on top of her, barely catching himself before he fell on her. His weight lightly pressed into her. Laughing, she put her hands over her head, breathing hard from the run.

"Only because I let you," he snarked, brushing hair from her face.

Flushing, Amy looked away from his intense gaze. "Want to meditate?" she asked, avoiding his eyes.

"Sure." He sat up and crossed his legs. She shook debris out of her ponytail and fixed her shirt. She scooted until she was sitting beside him, almost touching his leg with hers.

They meditated and tried to ignore their close proximity. Amy had a hard time clearing her mind as she tried to resist the urge to either scoot closer or further away, and she thought Connor might be having a similar experience. She almost sighed with relief when Connor said he thought they should move on to something else. She noted with a smirk that his cheeks were a bit more flushed than before. How odd to be training with the person she was supposed to fight. It felt oddly... natural.

They spent the rest of the evening trying to form their power into different shapes. Connor gave her a lot of pointers, and Amy was surprised to feel the Shield's approval as he taught her.

"*The Sword boy is quite skilled,*" the spirit said in her head, her tone thoughtful. Used to this sort of thing by now, Amy showed no outward sign of the conversation happening within.

"*Have you warmed up to him?*" she thought back, half listening to Connor explain how he made a cube.

"*I have.*" The spirit sounded confused. "*I have watched him through your eyes. He appears genuinely smitten with you. I have no doubt the Sword is against it, but he appears to be as natural at controlling it as you are at controlling me. Your abilities have progressed far beyond where you started.*" Amy dropped the partially formed cube she was holding. Connor looked at her with an eyebrow raised, but she waved him off with a smile and resumed.

"*It isn't like you to be so nice,*" she remarked.

"*I am merely stating the truth. I must rest. Continue your training with the Sword boy.*" The spirit's presence diminished in her mind.

Amy looked at her watch. It was already eight o'clock at night. "Shoot! I have to go home!" she exclaimed. "I didn't realize how late it was."

"I'll drive you," Connor said, releasing the energy he held in his hands.

"That's okay. It's honestly closer to walk than to go back to the car.

"Then I'll walk with you," he said, holding his elbow out to her like an old-fashioned gentleman. She smiled as she put her arm through his, hugging it to her and resting her head against his bicep.

"Fine, but it's silly. You'll have to walk all the way back to your car."

"Worth it," he said, kissing the top of her head. They walked in comfortable silence to the exit closest to Amy's apartment complex and to the foot of the stairs leading up to her apartment. The sun had set, and the outdoor lights were all on, casting deep shadows. Amy relished the contrast of Connor's warm skin against hers and the cold breeze blowing around them. The world was at that quiet point of settling in for the night, and the deep blue sky was speckled with bright stars.

"Thanks for walking me home," she said at last, letting Connor's arm go and feeling a pang at the loss of contact. "I should get going before Arty freaks out on me."

"No problem," he replied. "It was a nice walk." Stepping closer to her, he took her face in his hands and brought their lips together. Amy felt heat rush through her, and without thinking, she wrapped her arms around his neck, deepening the kiss.

They broke away, flushed. "Good night, Connor," she said, turning toward the stairs.

"Good night, Amy."

T HE NEXT MORNING, CONNOR DROVE TO AMY'S apartment to pick her up and waited for her at the bottom of the stairs. When she saw him, she threw herself at him and he caught her, then bent down to kiss her.

"Good morning," he said, beaming. Warmth always returned to him when they were together.

"Morning," she said, nestling her face into his chest. "Is this going to be a daily thing?" she asked, her voice muffled.

"That's my goal," he replied as he lifted her off the ground and shuffled them toward the car. She giggled and let go, landing on her feet before skipping to the car herself. Connor raced ahead and managed to put his hand on the door handle before she could. She pouted in response, and he smirked as he opened the door for her.

"I'll be faster than you someday," she warned, looking at him with narrowed eyes as she got inside.

"Sure you will." He laughed, closing her door and making his way over to the driver's side.

They continued to school, happily chatting the entire way. Connor parked and they made their way to the bus bay without incident. Amy held Connor's hand while simultaneously shifting through the crowd, dropping it suddenly when she saw Satomi and excitedly made her way toward her.

Connor followed her, half-smiling, but stopped when he felt a firm hand on his shoulder. His head snapped to the side, his eyes narrowing, to see Quinton and Peter standing there, Quinton jerking his hand back. Normal humans couldn't exactly feel the power Amy and Connor put off, but there was no mistaking the look on Connor's face.

"What do you want?" Connor snarled, turning to face the pair fully, internally wincing as they cringed away from him.

"Mr. Callaghan wanted us t-to check in on you," Peter mumbled, his voice low as his eyes darted around.

Connor glanced at Amy, who was watching him discreetly despite talking animatedly with Satomi and now Eric, who had just walked up and given Satomi a hug and a kiss. "And what does my father want?" he asked, turning his glare back on the cowering boys.

"He...he's worried that you're getting too...too close to the Shield girl," Quinton said, his eyes darting up to Connor's and back down.

"And why would he be worried about that?" Connor asked. He quickly threw on his charming smile as a boy from one of his classes came by and nodded in greeting. It dropped the second the boy was out of sight.

"Y-you keep leaving early and coming home late. And... and you seem..." Quinton trailed off. He started to tremble, causing Connor to mentally wince again. *Being a monster was much easier before Amy.*

"I seem what?" He kept his voice low, but harsh, as he had learned from his father.

"Um, well..." Peter struggled. "Happier?" He fidgeted with the hem of his shirt, seemingly quite interested in the ground.

Connor crossed his arms, then shifted his weight to his other foot. "Need I remind you idiots that I am supposed to get closer to her? That's what I am doing—I am getting closer to her."

"Y-your father wants you home on time today to speak with you," Quinton squeaked when Peter seemed unable to continue. Connor sighed and rolled his eyes.

"Fine, report back to him that I will go straight home after school." His voice was dismissive, and the boys immediately walked away, their shoulders slumping. Shaking his head, he turned to see Amy walking toward him with a look of concern. She slipped her hand in his again and started walking with him toward their next classes.

"Are you okay?" she asked, squeezing his hand.

He rolled his eyes as he played with her fingers in his. "Yes. My father wants to see me after school, so I won't be able to drive you home today."

"Will you be okay?" Amy was frowning, and Connor resisted the urge to touch her face.

He chuckled darkly. "Of course. He wants to check in on my progress of getting close to 'the Shield girl.'"

Her face paled, and Connor held her hand tighter as she drew closer to him. "What are you going to say?" she whispered so quietly that Connor could barely hear her.

"A twisted version of the truth."

As they reached Amy's classroom door, she hugged him more fiercely than usual, not letting go until the warning bell rang. She stood on her tiptoes to kiss him before saying, "It'll be okay, Connor. You can come over to my place or we can meet at the park afterward, if you want." She held his gaze.

He smiled and kissed her forehead, not wanting to worry her. "I'll text you when I can. Don't forget, we still have lunch together." She smiled back at him before heading off.

—

CONNOR ENTERED THE LUNCHROOM AND SAW Amy from behind, head whipping from side to side. He supposed he had been slightly later than normal.

"Hey, calm down," he said from behind her as he wrapped his arms around her waist. She yelped and jumped.

"Connor!" she exclaimed, covering her mouth with her hands. "You startled me."

He snorted. "Obviously. What's got you so worked up?" He led her to their table where Eric already sat, waving at them. Satomi was the only one who bought lunch, and she was already in line.

"Nothing, sorry." He looked down at her with a raised eyebrow. "Fine, I was just worrying about you is all."

He smiled, not replying because they were in earshot of Eric.

"Hey," Eric said brightly, setting out his lunch and then digging into a salad. "How have your days been?"

"Not bad," Amy said. She looked at him. He wasn't going to speak. She added, "Connor's been having an icky day though." He looked up at her and smiled slightly.

"Sorry to hear that, man. School or home?" Eric asked, looking genuinely concerned. Connor bristled slightly.

What would a normal teenager say? "Stupid parent stuff," he replied. He took out his lunch and picked at his sandwich noncommittally. It seemed dry and gross.

"Ah, I feel you there," Eric said sympathetically, not digging further.

He has no idea.

Satomi bounded over with her food and began her normal one-woman show of bad manners. Connor marveled at how someone so small could make such a huge mess every time they ate. He couldn't help but look at her a bit wistfully. *What would it be like to be that carefree? To be free at all?* His heart clenched.

"Connor?" Amy said, elbowing him lightly in the ribs. He jumped and looked at her.

"I'm sorry. What was it?" he asked, looking around to see everyone staring at him.

"Man, you are *out* of it," Eric remarked, causing Satomi

to bark out a laugh and a piece of french fry, which Connor did his best not to wince at.

"My apologies. I have been feeling a bit distracted today," he said running his hands through his hair and looking away from the table, doing his best not to make eye contact when he saw Peter and Quinton looking at him.

"That's okay," Amy said, patting him on the thigh. "Everyone gets distracted. We wanted to make sure you're okay." She looked meaningfully at him, knowing he couldn't share with the others.

He smiled, placing his hand on hers. "I'll feel better tomorrow, I'm sure." This seemed to appease the others, and Eric and Satomi began to chat again, Eric looking at her with complete adoration. Amy went back to eating, occasionally joining in, but mostly she watched Connor, who stayed quiet.

When the bell rang, they cleaned up the table. Connor threw away his half-eaten lunch. Satomi was already halfway to art class, and Eric had bid them farewell before heading to his class, but Amy stayed behind. *What if they make me stop seeing Amy altogether?*

"Hey, are you really okay?" she asked, putting a hand on Connor's shoulder. He was staring over the garbage can.

He turned and looked at her with a forced smile. "I am fine. Please, don't worry." Quinton and Peter were still watching from across the room.

With a forced show of exuberance, she wrapped her arms around his neck like usual and kissed him on the cheek before loudly saying, "See you later, Connor!" in a happy voice.

Connor winced and whispered, "You're a terrible actress." She shoved him by the arm and headed to art class, which made him laugh.

Turning, he faced Peter and Quinton and followed them to class, his mask firmly back in place.

34

Connor

QUINTON AND PETER HAD WATCHED HIM AS he got into his car, and he drove a bit slower than usual. The closer to the house he got, the colder he became. His stomach was churning and heavy like he'd swallowed a stone.

He left his car in the driveway and threw the keys at a man wearing a suit who was running toward him. Wordlessly, the man went to the car, got in, and drove it toward the detached garage. Connor headed to the front door, which opened for him almost automatically. Bertram gave him a half bow. *If only Bertram had been my real father.*

"Bertram." Connor nodded. Bertram was as polished as ever, but Connor thought he looked weary.

"Your father wishes to see you in his study," Bertram responded without preamble.

"Of course." Connor sighed before straightening his posture and heading off.

He knocked on the study door and waited until he heard, "Come in," to open it. He stepped in, closed the door behind him, and turned to face his father. His father sat behind his dark, spotless wooden desk, busily typing on a laptop. The only art that adorned the walls were fiery battle scenes painted in oils and framed in matching dark polished wood.

"Connor, have a seat," his father said without looking up. Connor pulled out a stiff-backed chair from in front of the desk and sat ramrod straight. Like everything else, the chair was made of the same dark wood. Preston's chair was a plush, deep brown leather and he wore a pressed black suit, dark gray tie, and black dress shirt. *He wants so badly to be the Sword host himself that he even dresses like its power.* After another moment of typing, he looked up at Connor. "Do you know why I've asked to see you?"

Connor kept eye contact, knowing that any sign of weakness would be akin to dropping blood in shark-infested waters. "I assume you're wanting a status report on my progress with the Shield girl." He kept his face and tone neutral.

Preston stood and walked around the desk, pacing the length of the room. When he turned back toward Connor, his face had a calm expression that Connor knew well. His palms started sweating, and his heart raced. He fought the urge to clench his hands and pressed his knees tightly together to keep them from shaking. The Sword stirred, sensing his fear, but he pushed it and his fear down. He was the Sword, not a child.

"Connor, I'm worried about you," Preston began. Connor kept his gaze focused on his father's eyes and kept his face impassive instead of letting out the derisive snort he wanted to. His eyes almost twitched as he avoided rolling them. When he didn't respond, Preston continued, "I'm worried that you've lost sight of the mission. Peter and Quinton have reported that you've been spending a lot of time with the Shield girl and that you've been acting quite differently. Why do you suppose they said that?"

Connor rolled his eyes this time. His disdain for the two boys was evident on his face and in his voice. "Perhaps because they're both too stupid to tell when I am acting and when I am not?"

Preston walked toward him, his calm face twisting. "Are you saying that they're wrong? That you're not falling for *that girl*?" Connor felt his jaw clench but didn't rise to the bait.

"You wanted me to get close to her, find weaknesses, and set up a betrayal. That's what I have done," Connor said in a bored tone. "The more effort I put into his, the stronger the emotional backlash will be."

"Yes, but I think you're getting too close to her. I want you to stop spending so much time with her. You're neglecting your studies and training. Besides, pulling away from her at this stage will probably be good for her destruction." Preston paced again.

"How could my studies and training be more important than this?"

"I am your father, and you will obey me," Preston said sharply, turning back toward Connor again. His eyes were hard, and his jaw was set. Connor saw color appear in his cheeks, a true warning sign.

"With all due respect, Father, I am the Sword's host, not you—" The back of Preston's hand came toward his face. Connor blocked it with his arm, and his chair fell backward as he stood quickly to tower over him. *When did I become taller than Father?*

"I am the Sword's host," Connor thundered, allowing the power of the Sword to enter his voice. "Not. You." Preston gaped, and his hand fell to his side. "I will do as I please. You are here merely to advise me and to provide me with the tools I need for my mission. Strike me again, *Father*, and I *will* strike back." Connor allowed his power to gather in his hand, causing it to glow with a gray light. His father stepped backward, his arms coming up defensively.

He waited, watching his father's face, then let his power recede. He picked up the chair and set it back before turning to face Preston. "Was there anything else?" Preston shook his head, speechless for the first time in Connor's life. Connor relished the paling of his face. "If that's all, I will take my leave." He left the room without looking back.

Connor walked out of the house and to the garage, not bothering to send someone for his car. He wanted nothing to do with any of the people his father employed. His hands were trembling, so he put them in his pockets until he reached the rack where the keys were all kept and grabbed his.

Finally, he got in, started it, and pulled out as quickly as he could. Putting his phone on Bluetooth, he called Amy. He knew she would be worried about him, which put a smile on his face. Being cared for by anyone other than Bertram was new to him, and it warmed him like the sun. But he didn't want her to feel bad, so he called her immediately.

The phone rang a few times before Amy picked up. "Connor?" she answered, her voice thick with concern and relief.

"Hey, Ames," he said, grinning. "Mind if I come over for a bit? Or we could go to the park?" He was hesitant to talk on a Sheath-provided cell phone more than necessary.

She hesitated.

"Is something wrong?"

"Well—"

"BOYFRIEND? HE'S YOUR *BOYFRIEND*?! I TRUSTED YOU TWO *ALONE!*" Arty was yelling.

Connor winced. "Ah," he said, not sure what else to say. "Should I... not come over?"

"Um," Amy started again. "HEY!"

Arty's voice came on instead, and Connor could hear Amy yelling in the background. "You can come over, but we're going to have a little heart-to-heart before pizza and games."

He blinked, almost missing a stop sign in his shock. "You still want me to come over?" He was completely out of his depth here.

"I can't say I'm thrilled that my sister is growing up and keeping *secret boyfriends* from me, but you don't seem like a bad guy," Arty said, then sighed. Connor barely kept himself from snorting. If only Arty knew. "Come over and we'll talk. Then we'll have fun."

"Uh, okay," Connor said as Arty hung up. His palms were sweating again and suddenly he was more terrified of a gangly nerd than his imposing father. *What if Arty says we can't be together? What will Amy do? What will I do?*

He was pretty sure that his stomach had actually tied itself into a pretzel by the time he got to their apartment complex.

"It's okay Connor, you've got this," he mumbled to himself in an unsure voice.

35

Amy

AMY PACED THE DINING ROOM, DREADING THE knock on the door she knew was coming. After Arty's initial blow-up, he'd calmed down. She hadn't anticipated his reaction because Arty seldom yelled about anything.

"Relax, Ames," Arty said as he walked into the dining room, running a hand through his hair. "I'm sorry I overreacted. I... I wasn't expecting this. One minute, you're a little thing who needs me for everything and the next, you're growing up." Amy looked over to see tears shining in his eyes.

"Oh, Arty," she said, running over to him and hugging him around the middle. "I'll always need you, even when I'm an adult."

Arty hugged her tightly. "I love you," he said, squeezing her tighter.

"I love you too, you giant dork."

Arty laughed and let her go, wiping his eyes. "I hope Connor doesn't think I'm a jerk." He resumed Amy's pacing while chewing on his thumbnail. She had to fight to keep from laughing.

"I'm sure he's fine," she said, waving a hand at him. As Arty opened his mouth to reply, there was a knock on the door. Arty paled as he took a deep breath and shook himself out. "Speak of the devil." She opened the door to see an equally pale Connor.

"Hi... Amy," he said, running a hand through his hair. His hair looked like he'd done that several times already, as it was standing up at odd angles. She looked at him, then back at Arty who also looked terrified, and she couldn't help herself. She laughed loudly and doubled over.

"You... two... are idiots." She gasped, breath fighting to enter her lungs. Straightening up with considerable effort, her eyes shone with tears, and she motioned Connor in. He and Arty made intense eye contact with each other, neither moving, and she burst out laughing again, the tears coursing down her cheeks as she wiped them off with the heel of her hand. "For goodness' sake, Connor." She grabbed him by the arm and dragged him in. "Come inside." She closed the door while they both stared at her, eyebrows raised. She turned to face them, barely controlling her laughter. "You're both so afraid of each other that I couldn't help but laugh. Connor, Arty is okay with us, and Arty, Connor is probably not... scared of you." The side of Connor's mouth twitched at that last statement.

Arty cleared his throat. "I probably could have handled that better," he said. "It came as a shock, and I wasn't ready."

Connor smiled. "Hey, it's no problem. I won't ever hurt her," he lied, looking right into Arty's eyes. "I really care about her." Amy knew exactly what he meant, and she felt her eyes burn with tears of a different type.

"You'd better not," Arty said, his tone serious. "I might not be very strong, but I will raise hell if you do." Connor nodded, his face serious. "So, what kind of pizza do we want tonight?" Arty walked toward the game closet, apparently deciding that the subject was closed.

Connor replied, "Uh... cheese? Veggie?" Amy snorted as she reached out and took his hand, pulling him into the living room. Arty grimaced when his eyes landed on their intertwined fingers, and Amy rolled her eyes.

"Grow up," she said, exasperated. "You've had boyfriends before too."

"That's different and watch your tone. I can still give you more of 'the talk' right here and now," he threatened, which made Amy and Connor laugh. In truth, he had given her as much of the talk as he could, and Mrs. Sanchez had, outside of school hours, helped with the rest. She helped Amy a lot when Arty had been completely lost on what to do and what to buy for her as she got older. Puberty had been a challenge for both of them. She shook her head to dispel the memories.

They settled in and spent the evening playing games and eating a deluxe veggie pizza. Connor, who didn't get pizza at home, ate with gusto. He wasn't a picky eater since he'd been brought up trying a lot of different food and had no issue eating vegetarian.

Around nine o'clock, Arty stood up and stretched. "Okay, it's bedtime. I missed my run today, so I have to get enough sleep to do it tomorrow." He looked around. "You two clean up, but no funny business!" He waggled his finger in front of Amy's face.

"Go to bed, nerd," she said, pushing his hand away and standing up as well. She began to gather plates.

"Uh, do you need any help?" Connor asked.

Amy stopped and looked at him. "Have you never had to clean up after yourself before?" She giggled, knowing she'd hit the nail on the head.

"Uh…"

"Here, I'll show you how us commoners do it." She gathered all of their plates and brought them to the kitchen, Connor trailing along behind her. "See? Not hard," she said, scrubbing the plates in the sink before putting them in the dishwasher. Then she gathered the garbage and put it in the garbage can. "Ta-da!" she said, throwing her hands up and turning toward him with flare like a magician.

He wrapped his arm around her waist, pulled her to him, and kissed her. "Very impressive," he said, his face inches from hers.

"I said no funny business!" Arty snapped as he came back in, causing them to jump apart. "You two are too funny." He grinned.

"C'mon, Connor, I'll walk you out to your car," she said, grabbing his hand and dragging him out of the apartment.

"Good night, Arty. Thank you for dinner," Connor called, waving. Arty returned the wave with a smile as he closed the door behind them.

Amy dragged Connor all the way to the stairwell and started descending it before he stopped her. "Hey, wait up," he said, pulling back.

She turned and grinned at him. "Sorry, I didn't want to hear any more sass from Arty," she said. "He can be such a baby about things."

"I can understand wanting to protect someone close to you," he said, staring into her eyes as he reached out to cup her face.

"What happened when you went home?" she asked, breaking the moment. Connor sighed and dropped his hand.

"They think I have been compromised," he said. "I put my dad in his place." He let out a shaky laugh. "I have never done that before."

"What did he do?" she asked quietly, reaching down to hold his hand.

"The usual. Yelled, blustered, et cetera. When he tried to backhand me, though, I stopped him and told him I am the Sword host, and I will be doing things my way."

Amy gasped, her face whitening. "He tried to hit you?" she asked in a choked whisper. He looked at her with a raised eyebrow.

"Well, yes. That is the way of the Sheath," he said with a shrug. "Obedience is everything." Amy threw herself against him and buried her face in his chest, hugging him as tightly as she could.

"I'm so sorry, Connor!" Her voice was muffled.

He put a hand on the back of her head as he hugged her back. "It's okay, really. It's not something that I will be allowing anymore," he said darkly. She looked up at him with shining eyes. "Don't cry, it's not like you did anything."

She pulled away, rubbing her eyes. "I know, but it's so sad. I can't imagine being hurt by Arty. The worst he's ever done is ground me for a couple weeks and take away my art supplies."

Connor barked out a laugh. "What could you have possibly done to make him so angry?"

She looked up at him sheepishly. "I got caught in a lie about school. Lying is a big no-no in our house, and he wasn't happy. The worst part was the 'I'm-very-disappointed-in-you' guilt trip that came with it." She faked a shudder. "It did teach me not to lie ever again. Well… until now." She made a quick orb of light form in her palm before immediately crushing it in her fist.

"Do you think you'll ever tell him?"

Amy sighed. "I don't want to. He'd try to stop my training, and he certainly wouldn't want me seeing *you* ever again."

"Do you blame him?" Connor asked, his voice full of self-loathing. "We are going to kill each other."

"We'll cross that bridge when it gets here," Amy said with a shrug. "Until then, I want to live every day as fully as I can." She kissed him quickly before releasing him and starting back down the stairs. "You'd better leave before Arty comes out screaming about 'funny business' and embarrasses us in front of the whole complex. Are you okay to go home? Will you be alright?"

They reached the bottom of the stairs, and Connor's car was only a few feet away. He nodded at her question. "I'll be fine, I always am. I will see you bright and early in the morning for school." He took her face in both of his hands, leaning down to kiss her. She wrapped her arms around his neck, holding him tightly, relishing the warmth that flooded her body.

After what felt like forever, but was only a few seconds, they pulled apart.

"Good night, Amy," he said as he walked to his car.

"Good night, Connor," she said, turning and walking back up the stairs. She looked down and watched him until his car was out of sight.

36
Preston

PRESTON REACHED ACROSS HIS DESK TO GRAB the handset of his phone. The phone had been high-end at one point but had since become dated. He dialed and waited.

"Sir?" a voice answered on the other end after only two rings.

"Schedule the other elders for a conference call as quickly as possible and bring Quinton and Peter to the estate immediately." Preston hung up. He paced the room, brows furrowed, and shoulders hunched. After about thirty minutes, there was a knock on the door. Preston sat behind his desk, smoothed back his hair, and said, "Enter."

The door opened to reveal the tall, broad form of Connor's driver, Roland, with Peter and Quinton behind him. Both boys looked down at the ground, their legs trembling slightly.

"Boys, come in. I will need you momentarily." Peter and Quinton shuffled in. Preston looked on in disgust as Peter sucked in his tummy and Quinton looked like he was trying to curl in on himself. They stood against the wall near the door. Roland glanced at Preston, who gave him a dismissive wave, before closing the door and leaving.

Preston walked over to a bookshelf and ran his hand along the spines before stopping at a black one with silver embellishments. He tugged on the book and pulled the entire bookcase out like a door, revealing the entrance to a small, dark room. He reached in to flick on a light, which illuminated the confined space. The walls were white and unadorned. It was less stately than his office and only contained a small bookcase, a desk, and a monitor large enough to be a TV mounted to the wall. The bookcase contained a collection of old, brittle-looking books and a few scrolls—the Sheath's most ancient collection of knowledge.

Preston walked into the small room and took a seat at the desk, powering on the machine, and waiting for the screen to come to life. Multiple darkened silhouettes appeared when it did.

"Fellow Elders, we have a problem," he began without preamble. "The host needs some... encouragement to fulfill his duties. He has become too close to the Shield girl. I propose we perform the control ceremony."

"The ceremony would be an intensive and risky undertaking. What proof have you of this claim?" came a slightly distorted voice. The speaker's voice was masked by software, but the name "Elder F" was visible.

"Today, he deliberately disobeyed orders and left to see her again. He is with her often. We have eyewitness testimony from the two boys assigned to be his companions. It was they who first alerted us to these changes."

"We would like to question the witnesses. Performing the ceremony may harm the vessel and could weaken the Sword's return. It should not be undertaken lightly." This voice was different from the first, but also distorted.

"Boys, come in," Preston barked. The boys scurried into the room and stood with their backs against the wall furthest from him. "Come closer, the elders wish to question you. Do not forget what will happen to you and your families if you lie." His tone was harsh, and the boys moved behind him, both glancing at the screen. All that could be seen were the blacked-out profiles of five people with plain, gray backgrounds.

"You are his assigned companions?" the first voice asked.

Quinton's face went pale, and he swayed.

Peter gulped and looked at the screen. "Yes, sir," he whispered.

"Speak up, boy," Preston snapped, lifting his hand menacingly. Both flinched.

"Yes, sir," Peter said louder. "Yes, s-sir, we are the assigned c-companions to the host vessel."

"What does your assignment entail?" the second voice asked.

Peter glanced at Quinton, who looked like he was turning green. Peter gulped and faced the screen, speaking for them both. His cowardice was befitting one so low. "W-we are assigned to all of C-Connor—I mean the vessel's, classes. We observe him and p-play the role of his f-friends in public. We accompany him on any outings where it would be inappropriate for a-a person of his caliber to be alone. We report anything out of the ordinary to our p-parents, who then report back to M-Mr. Callaghan." Peter flinched at the last part.

"A very prized assignment," the first voice said.

Quinton swallowed hard and looked at Peter.

"Yes, sir. We are very proud to s-serve the Sheath in any capacity they require," Quinton said weakly as sweat beaded on his forehead.

"What did you report that led to this meeting?"

Peter and Quinton exchanged panicked looks before unwillingly looking to Preston for guidance.

Preston pinched the bridge of his nose. *Incompetents, the lot of them.* "Tell them how he changed, imbeciles."

"Yes, sir," Peter responded. He spoke in a rush, losing his fearful stammer in his haste. "When Connor—I mean the host vessel first met Am—the Shield girl, he treated her like he treats most people at school as befitting a person of his station. He has always been... formal, but polite, with our classmates again, as is befitting one of such an exalted station." Peter carried on, "After some time with her, he began to dismiss us to talk to her privately. At first, we assumed he was making her feel more comfortable but later he... he ch-changed." Peter stopped and stared at Quinton again.

"Changed how?" came another distorted voice on the call.

"He seems happier," Quinton blurted.

"Happier?"

"H-he laughs with the girl. He has distanced himself from us. The way he speaks of the Sheath has felt less...

committed? He hasn't said anything directly seditious, but he has become a totally different person." Quinton's hands shook visibly.

"Hmmm. Elder Host Father, have you noticed anything?"

"Not directly, Fellow Elder. I have not seen my son with the Shield girl, but I have noticed him distancing himself and being less committed to his studies. He spends more time out of the house than he did before. It's been reported by watchers that he spends his time with the Shield girl in the park and at her home. We cannot get too close without him knowing he is being watched, but I do not believe he is a committed host any longer."

There were a few moments of silence. "This is a very grave accusation indeed. You feel the ceremony is the only way to ensure victory?"

"I do."

"We shall vote upon it. All in favor of commencing with preparations for the ceremony, raise your hands." All five profiles on the screen raised theirs, as did Preston. "Very well. Elder Host Father, make preparations on your end. We will come to you when it is time."

Preston's face broke out in a slow, triumphant grin. "Yes, Fellow Elder, I shall. Thank you all for meeting today. We will achieve the Sword's ultimate goal, for we are the Sheath."

"We are the Sheath," the five distorted voices said in unison before the monitor went black.

Preston looked at Peter and Quinton. "What are you still doing here?"

They recoiled.

"What you have witnessed here shall remain a secret, do you understand?"

They nodded emphatically.

"Good. Your families have been rewarded for your services. If you don't want the rewards or your lives to end, you will continue with your assignment and speak to no one of this. Only the inner-most members may know. If word gets out, I will know it was from the two of you." Preston turned back to the computer. "Now get out and have someone drive you home."

Peter and Quinton fled the office, closing the door quietly behind them, as Preston resumed his pacing.

37

Amy

AMY DASHED OUT THE DOOR, DOWN THE STAIRS, and straight into Connor's arms. The cold December air bit at their bundled-up forms as their breath fogged the air around them. She smiled up at him and noticed there were circles under his eyes and their normally vibrant emerald color looked dull. He was pale and sallow, but his tailored clothes still looked nice, though they were slightly too big on him.

"Are you getting enough sleep?" Amy asked as she rummaged around in her backpack to double-check for her homework after getting in the car. She'd raced Connor to the door to try to open it first, but he'd won, as always. Darn short legs.

He sighed. "For the one-thousandth time, yes. I get at least eight hours every night." He ran his hand through his hair. "I just haven't been sleeping *well*."

"Connor, you haven't been sleeping well for an entire month, since before Thanksgiving." She looked up at him with concern. "Have you gone to a doctor yet?"

He shook his head. "I've just been having a lot of weird dreams."

"What kind of dreams?"

Connor shuddered slightly. "Ugly ones."

"What kind of 'ugly'?" she prompted when he didn't elaborate.

"I don't know... *ugly*. They're foggy, and I can't remember anything. I only remember darkness, but not the darkness of sleep."

Amy's eyes widened. "You don't think it's the Sword, do you?"

He shook his head again. "I asked the acolytes, and they said that the Sword doesn't affect the host's dreams. They gave me some weird potions to try and help my energy, but they didn't do anything."

"Do you trust them?"

Connor laughed harshly. "Not as far as I can throw them. Though, come to think of it, I bet I could throw them pretty far." Amy giggled. "But they won't do anything to hurt their precious host. The Sword is too important to them."

"I suppose," she replied skeptically. She made a mental note to talk to the Shield today. The Shield had been mostly dormant since October, only emerging occasionally to help with her training. The Shield seemed... tired. Could a spirit get tired? She'd asked it, but it had brushed her off.

Connor and Amy hung out with Satomi and Eric at the beginning of the day like always, then again at lunch.

Eric was too friendly not to be liked, and Satomi and him were adorable together. He was completely wrapped around her oblivious finger. Satomi was a wild, free spirit, but Eric seemed to like that about her. He seemed content to watch her fly.

AT THE END OF THE DAY, AMY AND CONNOR walked with Satomi out to the bus bay. She ran toward her bus and, while on the bottom stair, turned around and called, "Amy, don't forget to be at my house by six o'clock if you want dinner. You know how my mom is about timing." She rolled her eyes.

Amy laughed. "Of course, how could I ever forget *that*? I'm stoked to come spend the night and get a whole Saturday with you!" She waved as Satomi's driver rushed her the rest of the way onto the bus.

Holding hands, Connor and Amy walked through the school and out the front to Connor's car. As they neared the car, there was a brief scuffle as Amy sprinted to open the door herself.

"What will you do tonight?" she asked as Connor buckled himself in. "Miss me?"

Connor snorted. "Of course I will, but I'm a strong, independent man."

She laughed. "Keep telling yourself that." She sobered. "You'll go to bed early?"

"If you insist."

38
Connor

BICKERING PLAYFULLY, THEY MADE THEIR WAY back to Amy's apartment. He dropped her off with a quick kiss before heading to his house, as his father wanted him home on time. As he got closer and closer to the estate, he became more tired, drained even.

By the time he pulled into the driveway, he was having trouble keeping his eyes open. As he placed the car into park, weakness and dizziness swamped him. He stumbled out and landed hard on the cold ground.

"Mr. Connor!" He heard Bertram's voice coming as if from a distance. Soon, he was rolled onto his back and felt a hand on his forehead. "Connor, can you hear me?"

Connor opened his eyes to see Bertram's worried face above him, wrinkles suddenly standing out in stark clarity. His deep brown eyes were wide and terrified.

"Bertram," he croaked. "I don't—"

Bertram was shoved harshly out of the way.

"Move!" Preston came into view.

"Father..." Connor felt like he was fading. His limbs tingled and everything seemed fuzzy.

"Bring him downstairs," his father snarled. "He's ready for the ceremony."

"Mr. Callaghan, shouldn't we call for an ambulance?" Bertram asked in a strained voice. Connor could hear what sounded like many footsteps coming toward him, but they sounded somehow underwater.

"No, we've been waiting for this," Preston said. Connor could barely hear them anymore, but he could feel hands carrying him.

Several black-robed figures carried the barely conscious Connor into the house, through a hallway, and down a flight of stairs hidden behind a panel that blended in with the rest of the wall. Connor had never seen it before. The air was colder, and the smell of something damp almost overwhelmed his senses. A low sort of humming came from somewhere ahead, and the sound made his skin crawl. Goose bumps sprang up on his arms as his stomach became heavy. Something was wrong. He could feel it in his soul.

The Sword swirled inside of him and Connor could almost feel its glee. He tried to move his arms to free himself, but nothing happened. He tried to call on his power, but a wall had formed in front of it that he couldn't breach. Cold sweat broke out across his forehead as his breathing became fast and shallow. *What's happening? Am I dying?*

Finally, he felt himself being carefully lowered onto a frigid, hard slab. He struggled to open his eyes. Darkness pressed in from above him, barely broken by the flickering light of candles. The humming sound he had heard before was louder here, like some kind of low chant. He couldn't place the language, but it chilled him further.

Exerting every ounce of willpower he had left, Connor turned his head to the side and forced his eyes open. He saw a row of five crimson-robed acolytes, faces hidden and kneeling in a circle around him. A few black-robed acolytes lined the wall behind them. He could tell there was a symbol etched into the floor, but he couldn't make it out as his vision blurred. He realized with a stab of dread that he had never been in this room before. He could only make out part of it, but he had never seen it in his studies or in his time living here.

"He's ready." Connor's father was above him again. Preston wore a wicked grin on his face. And, like the others closest to Connor, he wore a robe of deep crimson.

"Father…?" Connor groaned.

"Shut up, boy. Think you can disobey me? Think you can go against the might of the Sword *and* the Sheath? We have ways of dealing with unruly hosts like you." He left Connor's view for a moment, and Connor heard the clanking of bottles before smelling something acrid in the air. He coughed. His limbs were heavy, and his mind was growing fuzzier.

The Sword was moving around inside of him, faster and faster. He couldn't tell why he was blocked from his power, but he assumed it wasn't good.

"What…?" Just saying one word was an immense effort.

"I'm surprised you can still talk," his father noted clinically from somewhere to Connor's left. "We've spent the last two months slowly weakening you. As I said, we have ways of dealing with unruly hosts." Connor felt something sharp stab him in the arm, followed by a wave of cold spreading through the limb. "You are not the first host to try to fight fate," Preston continued conversationally. "None have fought as long as you, though. This should have only taken a few weeks, but everyone can be worn down eventually. Your body truly was made to be the perfect host for the Sword."

The coldness spread to Connor's shoulder. Something was very, very wrong, and fear crept up his throat as tears burned in his eyes. His finger twitched, but he hadn't been the one to will it to move.

"It's finally working." Preston's face came into Connor's view again, this time with a wide grin on it. "You see, boy, the Sword has been watching the Shield girl through your eyes this whole time, and it thinks the time to strike has come. But we know how much you... care... for the girl." His father said the word *care* with a grimace as if it was something disgusting. He chortled, a most unsettling sound. "It knows her weakness. You see, it has ways of communicating with those who are most loyal."

The coldness spread into his chest and neck. He tried to move again but felt like he was paralyzed. He slammed his will against the wall between him and his power and heard the Sword roar at him in a feral screech inside of his head.

"Now, now, Connor, be a good boy like we trained you to be. Give in to the Sword. It wants your body and after all, this is what you were born for." His father sounded unhinged. "I was so proud when I learned that I was the father of the latest host." He walked out of sight, but Connor could hear his voice joining in with the chanting. Tears spilled down his face, into his hair.

I wish I'd stayed with Amy longer. He closed his eyes and pictured hers. He loved to lose himself in her blue eyes. *I don't want to do this. I don't want to kill her! I love her.* Clenching his eyes closed, he concentrated with all his might on stopping the spread of ice through his body. For a moment, it halted, and he heard the Sword scream inside of him, then felt it bash against his mind.

"Chant louder! He's fighting it!" Preston screeched. The chanting around him swelled and soon was loud enough to drown out his thoughts. The chants echoed around and around the room, filling his every pore with the sound.

At long last, the chill reached his head and his heart simultaneously. "Amy," he whispered as the world went black and all was encased in ice.

39
Preston

ONNOR'S BODY SAT UP JERKILY, HIS HEAD LOLL-ing back and rolling against his shoulders. The chanting halted, and the robed figures fell forward and pressed their faces to the floor in supplication. Except for Preston, who sat on folded legs, staring at what was left of his son with a grin. Tears streamed down his face unchecked as he stared, transfixed, at his god.

Connor's body stretched and moved robotically to swing its legs over the side of the table. "*Preston,*" a voice hissed from Connor's mouth.

"Yes, my lord?" Preston scrambled over to the body on his hands and knees, not even feeling the scrape of the stone. "What do you need?" Connor's hand shot out and grabbed Preston's throat. He made a strange, gurgling sound, but didn't fight back other than to grab at the wrist that held him to steady himself. His throat hurt, but he was still able to breathe.

"*You have done well, Preston.*" Connor's head snapped toward him and his mouth spread into a wide grin, too wide for Connor's actual mouth. Preston blinked wildly but made no move to free himself. He stared, transfixed, into what used to be emerald eyes. Instead, they were pitch black and glowing with a strange, gray light. The Sword released Preston, who fell back coughing and clutching at his throat.

"Thank you, my lord," he croaked. The bodies of all the robed figures around them trembled but did not otherwise move.

The Sword looked at its new hand and a ball of flickering black and gray energy formed there. It moved its gaze to the other hand and formed another ball of energy, then it clenched its hands and the energy vanished. "*This body will do nicely,*" it murmured, looking down at itself. A surge of pride raced through Preston.

"*It is time to destroy the Shield once and for all. She is barely conscious anymore, and besting the Shield girl will be simple. It is finally my time.*" Connor's body flew up and out the door, through the house, and straight through the closed front door.

40
Amy

AMY WAS PAINTING HER NAILS AS THEY watched Satomi's favorite anime. It was a show about a bunch of rich high school boys running a host club. Amy wasn't as big of an anime fan as Satomi was, but she did love this show.

Amy looked over at Satomi. She had her hair piled in a messy bun on top of her head, a green face mask on, and was painting each nail a different neon color, much like her walls, which were jam-packed with art and posters. They had decided to have the girliest girls' night possible, hitting every single cliché they could think of.

"How are you and Eric doing?" Amy asked as she painted another coat of sky blue on her nails. She inhaled deeply, and the air still smelled like the chocolate chip cookies they'd baked earlier.

Satomi sighed dreamily. "Great! I like him a lot. He's so nice and smart—I never thought I'd date someone so... normal, but he gets me. He doesn't laugh at my clothes or the things I like. He's even starting to watch some of my favorite shows, and he seems to actually like them!" She smiled. "What about you and Connor?"

Amy sighed, adding a coat of gold sparkles to each of her ring fingers. "We're doing great, but I'm worried about him. He hasn't been looking so good lately." She paused to blow on her nails and inspected the effect of adding the gold. "His family isn't the nicest, so that isn't helping."

"That sucks," Satomi said, adding silver glitter to her nails. "I've noticed the same thing. He's been looking rough for a few weeks."

"I hope it isn't anything too bad." She flopped backward onto Satomi's bed with her hands up in the air and her fingers spread to protect her nails from getting smudged. Satomi's multi-colored comforter was soft beneath her.

They chatted for a while longer before starting to play some old sleepover games. They were in the middle of M.A.S.H. when Amy's phone started to vibrate. She picked it up and saw that it was a number she didn't recognize with the local area code. Something told her she should answer.

"Hello?" she said as she took the call.

"Is this Amy Sanders?" came a gruff, male voice.

"Yes, who's calling?"

"This is Dr. Stephens. Are you a relative of Arthur Sanders? You were the name listed in his phone's emergency contacts." Amy sat up, her body suddenly going ice cold. Everything blurred around her.

"Yes, I'm his sister," she answered.

Satomi looked up at her with alarm. Amy's eyes were wide, her face drained of color.

"Can you come to Whittaker General? We need to speak with you about your brother." The doctor's voice was professional and calm, which did absolutely nothing to calm Amy.

"What happened? Is he okay?" Her voice came out sounding strangled. Satomi got up to sit beside her and put an arm around her shoulders—she had started to shake.

"Your brother is in surgery—"

"Surgery?!" Amy almost shrieked. Satomi jumped.

"Yes ma'am. We can tell you more if you come down to the hospital. I don't think his life is in danger, but we need to speak with you right away."

"I'll be right there."

"Just come to the front desk and ask for Dr. Stephens." Amy hung up the phone. She felt her power swirling inside of her, and it was a struggle to contain it.

"Ames, what's wrong?" Satomi asked, her voice quavering. Amy grabbed her mini backpack and ran out of the room and down the stairs.

"*The Sword has made its move. It is time.*" The Shield's voice rang through her mind, causing Amy's stomach to try to escape.

"*What do you mean?*" Amy sniped back at it as she ran toward the front door. Satomi's parents stood up from the couch, clearly alarmed.

"Amy, are you okay?" Mrs. Yamada asked, her face concerned.

"Something happened to Arty. I have to go," she replied as she unlocked the front door.

"Where are you going this late at night?" Mr. Yamada had moved to stand beside his wife, putting an arm around her shoulders. His messy style clashed wildly with Mrs. Yamada's polished one.

"The hospital," Amy said, already halfway out the door.

"Let us drive you," he said, starting to walk toward her.

"Sorry, can't." *I don't have time for cars or questions.*

"Amy, you can't go out alone this late at night!" But she was already sprinting out of sight. "Amy!" he yelled after her. She ran toward the hospital, channeling her power into her legs to strengthen them, keeping to areas where there would be fewer people.

"Okay," she said out loud. "What do you mean 'it's time'?"

"*I can feel it. The Sword is on the move. It has made the first strike.*"

"The first strike?" she asked, confused as she took a sharp turn. "Arty?" Nausea almost choked her, but she swallowed hard and kept running, her heart pounding in her ears.

"*I think so. Amy Sanders, you need to be ready. When you see the Sword boy, he will not be who you know anymore.*"

"What do you mean?" she panted.

"*The Sheath have ways of making an unwilling host submit to the Sword. I'm sure you've felt me fading in and out over the last several months. We are weaker with every incarnation, which is why you have the power to push me aside. In the beginning, we completely controlled our hosts once we*" *were inside of them. Now, we are shadows of our former selves. It's why your training was so important. Because you will be facing the Sword, not me."*

Amy's limbs tingled and her breathing picked up. She halted, taking quick, shallow breaths. She placed her hands on her knees, and her whole body shook. Helplessness consumed her as the panic attack swept over her. She rubbed her hands together, forcing herself to breathe and start running again. Running would help, so long as she could force herself to do it.

"What are you saying?" she asked. "What do you mean?"

"I mean, Amy Sanders, that tonight... you will fight."

Finally, the hospital came into view. "Fine, but I need to see Arty first."

She could almost feel the Shield thinking as she neared the front entrance. *"I believe you have time. The Sword would have wanted this, to get you off balance."*

Amy almost crashed into the automatic doors in her rush to get inside. She came to a jerky stop as she recalled the power from her legs. Her breathing was uneven, and sweat slid down her face.

She walked as fast as she could to the front desk where a woman with brown hair and pink scrubs sat in front of a computer. The woman opened her mouth to speak, but Amy cut her off. "Please," she panted. "I need to see Dr. Stephens."

The nurse's face held a pitying expression, which caused Amy's insides to twist. "What's your name?" she asked in a kind voice.

"Amy Sanders. I'm here for my brother, Arty, Arthur Sanders." She started to twist the hem of her sweater, finding it hard to hold still.

"I'll page Dr. Stephens right now," the woman said, picking up the phone. Amy stood there, fighting the urge to scream at the poor woman helping her. After she hung up, she asked, "Do you have an ID?"

Amy pulled her backpack to the front and took out her wallet. "Would a school ID work? I don't have my license yet," she said, taking out the card.

"It should. How old are you?" the lady asked as she held out her hand.

"Seventeen," Amy replied, handing her the ID.

"Do you have parents or any adults we could call?"

Amy had never wished for her parents to be alive more than in this very instant. She couldn't handle this, she couldn't. Suddenly, she was once more the scared little girl crying for her parents that would never come home. She swallowed. "No, it's just us. We don't have any family."

The nurse gave her a soft look and typed on her computer. "Dr. Stephens will be here in a minute. Why don't I show you to the family waiting room?"

Amy followed the lady to a closed-off area with lots of chairs, magazines, and some toys. Fortunately for her, it was empty. It was early evening, and she figured visiting hours were probably over. She started pacing, agitated, as soon as the woman walked away. Every minute felt like an agonizing eternity.

"Ms. Sanders?" Amy turned to see a middle-aged man with a kind face walking toward her. He had on a white doctor's coat with black slacks and black shoes on. His hair was short and dark brown with some hints of gray in it.

"Dr. Stephens?" she croaked, taking a shaky step toward him.

"Yes, you got here much faster than I expected."

"I was close by. Where is Arty?"

"We can talk in my office."

"No, take me to my brother *right now*." It was all she could do to keep her power in check, but some of it echoed in her strained voice. Dr. Stephens shook his head.

"He's still in surgery, it would be very dangerous for him if you were to barge in there."

Amy stared at him, feeling her eyes welling up with tears again. "Fine, tell me what's wrong." Dr. Stephens led her to an office. They passed rooms with people in them, but she could take in nothing other than the back of his white coat. The sounds of the hospital blended in her ears, creating a low hum.

"Amy, how old are you?" he asked once they were seated. His office was a warm beige color with framed diplomas on the wall behind him and nature scenes on the other walls. Amy fidgeted in a low-backed chair despite the room's calming aura.

"Seventeen. What happened?"

"Do you have anyone you can call? Parents, perhaps? Yours was the only phone number in the emergency contacts on his phone."

"They're dead. I already answered these questions," she said harshly, struggling to keep her power in check. "It's just us. Tell me what happened." Dr. Stephens sighed and settled back into his chair, his face becoming a professional mask.

"Honestly, we're not sure. Some joggers found your brother unconscious in the park a little bit ago. He looked like he'd been thrown into a tree trunk with force, though we're not sure how that could be possible. He is still alive, but some of the scans we did seem concerning."

"What do you mean?"

"There appears to be some soft tissue damage and swelling around his spine."

"His spine?" Amy said in a whisper, feeling as if the ground beneath her was opening up.

"We don't think he's in immediate danger, but he won't be able to leave the hospital anytime soon. We need to see if there was damage to the spinal cord. He was unconscious, but we didn't see anything on any of the scans to indicate a brain injury."

She didn't speak right away, and tears flowed down her cheeks. "When will we know?" she finally managed to say, her voice sounding far away in her ears.

Dr. Stephens looked at her with sympathy. "In a few hours, but even then, it might take some time to know the full extent of the damage. Your brother is young and appears to be quite healthy, both of which are very good things."

"He was almost done training for a marathon he qualified for," she whispered, looking blankly at the desk. "He needs to be able to run. The race is in a few weeks. He can't be stuck here. He can't be... paralyzed. He needs to run. He loves running." She felt a sob building in her chest but suppressed it. Dr. Stephens stood up, walked around the desk, and kneeled in front of her.

"Amy, no one has said paralyzed yet. We have some great

surgeons working here, and your brother is young. Don't give up hope yet. There is still a chance he'll recover. We just need time. Is there someone I can call to wait with you?"

Amy rubbed her eyes. "No, I need to go. Please call me when he's out of surgery." A deep burning rage started to overcome the tears. The Sword had gone after her brother. Her brother. Her nerdy, funny, loud, loving, wonderful brother. Her brother was in surgery. How *dare* that thing touch her *brother*.

"Miss Sanders, you've had quite a shock. I think it would be best if—" Dr. Stephens started to say, but Amy stood suddenly, her vision blazing gold for part of a second. The doctor flinched and rubbed his eyes.

"I have to go," she repeated, then sprinted out of the hospital. She heard gasps as she ran by and heard someone yell at her for running, but she didn't care. She ran through the doors that were opening as someone walked in, and she plunged out into the night.

She opened herself to her powers, allowing them to flow freely through her body. The Shield was awake and alert, guiding her. Words weren't needed, not when they were as one.

Amy could feel the Sword's power, it wasn't even trying to hide. She ran as fast as she could in its direction, unsurprised when she found herself charging through the barriers indicating that Whittaker Hills Park was closed. The barriers crumpled under her power.

At last, she came to the clearing where she trained and where she and Connor had spent so much time together. She came to a halt, her breathing even.

Connor was standing in the middle of the clearing, arms crossed and smirking. She stopped at the edge. His skin looked gray, his eyes glowed a strange black, and his mouth looked wrong, like it was somehow too big for his face.

"What have you done with Connor?" she thundered, her power bursting around her. Her eyes glowed gold, and her ponytail blasted backward from the force of her power.

Connor opened his arms to her. "*I'm right here, Amy.*" His voice sounded distorted and monstrous. Goose bumps rose along her arms.

A lump formed in her throat, but she ignored it. There was no time to mourn. "You're not Connor," she said, her voice firm. She would mourn later, if there was a later.

"*No, but I am as close to him as you will ever get again. He is gone, buried inside me.*" The thing pointed Connor's hand at his temple. "*He is asleep, and he will never reawaken. Did you like my present?*" the voice hissed, the grin somehow becoming even bigger.

"Present?"

"*Your brother. He tried to fight me, but he was no match of course. It was like throwing a child.*" The monster threw its head back and laughed a horrible, twisted sound.

Amy stood firm, her hands balling into fists, and her power flowed even faster around her. Red started to cloud her vision, and a white-hot rage coursed through her like lava. "You did that to him? You hurt Arty?" she asked, fists shaking with rage. Who else could it have been? But hearing that thing take ownership of it...

"*Yes,*" it purred. "*It was fun. I hurt your precious brother using your boyfriend's body.*"

Amy felt something deep inside of her snap. She propelled herself forward with all the power she could muster, launching herself at the monster with a snarl so loud it echoed throughout the clearing.

41

Amy

The Sword had known full well that she would snap and had been ready. As she flew toward it, it threw up a wall of gray power. Amy shot a bolt of golden energy through the wall, causing it to shatter. Before she knew what she was doing, she punched its face, her rage overpowering her.

Sword or not, this was still Connor's body and he had trained it for years. The Sword caught her wrist, pulled her in, and hit her on her back. Her mouth flew open as she crashed toward the ground. She threw her power beneath herself to stop her fall, then broke his grip as she'd been trained. The monster laughed as she flew back, panting already.

"You are quite possibly the weakest Shield host I've ever fought." Amy wiped the sweat from her face and threw a ball of energy. Her thoughts were all over the place, and she

couldn't focus enough to bring her power to bear properly. The Sword batted it away, laughing. *"It looks like you will be the first Shield in history to break."*

It stalked toward her.

Amy threw ball after ball of energy at it, but nothing hit. Her breath came out in weak gasps, the air barely able to enter her lungs.

In a flash, the monster was in front of her. It broke her guard and picked her up by the throat, holding her above the ground before starting to fly upwards.

The Shield screamed at her from somewhere in her mind, but she couldn't understand it. It tried desperately to take control, but her emotions blocked it. She looked down into the black eyes set in the face of the monster before her when suddenly, they flashed emerald. For an instant, Connor's eyes showed through, and she could see the terror and despair in them.

"Connor," she croaked out, clinging to his wrist and trying to pull away.

Once more, the Sword laughed, its mouth stretching and distorting. *"Connor is gone. I already told you that, you stupid little girl."* It hoisted her up higher before throwing her toward the ground.

"Connor," she wheezed as she formed a bubble of golden light around herself, stopping her descent. His emerald eyes became her whole world, grounding her in the moment. The Sword spiraled downward at her and slammed its glowing fist into her sphere She put both hands in front of her, overlapping them, and held firm. "CONNOR!" she yelled. "Connor, I know you're in there! You have to fight it! I can't lose you!"

The shrieking cackle of the Sword pierced her ears. "*He is gone, but you will see him soon!*" The monster struck the shield around her over and over. The blows reverberated through her, but she held steady, picturing Connor's eyes. She closed her own eyes, keeping her hands out in front of her, and concentrated on Connor. She reached out with her mind, using her power to push toward the beast in front of her, entering its mind. Nothing would keep her from Connor.

At first, all she could feel was the Sword. Her mind felt its presence, which was terrifying. It was chaos tinged with an overwhelming desire for destruction. The Sword noticed her intrusion, and the blows she felt around her orb halted.

"*You think you'll do better in here?*" it whispered. Amy realized she was no longer in her body, rather she was instead surrounded by intense darkness. All she could see ahead of her was a pair of hideously glowing eyes and the jagged line of a mouth.

"Connor!" she called out again, ignoring the monster and surrounding her form with golden light. She started to walk, hands held in front of her. "Connor, where are you?" There wasn't anything below her, but somehow, she was still able to walk in this strange place.

Dark gray light swirled around her, pushing in on her. It felt as if she would be suffocated into nothingness. "*I am a spirit.*" The Sword's voice was all around her, feeling like a thousand needles pricking at her skin. "*Yet you try to fight me on the spiritual plane? This is a first. Unprecedented.*"

Halting, she closed her eyes and moved her legs to cross under her as she floated in the nothingness. Her breath felt cool against her nose, and she inhaled deeply, focusing on finding Connor. She had to focus with more effort than she'd ever used before to get past the dark energy and pain overtaking her. Connor was all that mattered, and she'd take down the spirit on its home turf to get him back.

The Sword howled, trying to overwhelm her, but she held on. The spirit pulled at her desperately, trying to take over and fight. She ignored its attempts and thought about Connor. His awkward smile flashed in her mind. The blush he got when he was taken by surprise. The warmth of his arms around her. The warmth of his lips on hers. It felt real as she pulled the memories to the surface. Her intense feelings swelled inside her, contrasting with the pressure from the spirit.

She needed to tell him she loved him. *Why didn't I tell him a long time ago?*

"Connor," she breathed. A concussive wave of golden energy radiated out from her, pushing back the darkness. The Sword screamed as it was blown away from her.

Glowing, she uncrossed her legs and stood as she opened her eyes. There was something in the distance—a weak glimmer. Every part of her was pulled toward that glimmer. She floated toward it, her power shimmering around her.

"*I am still he-re!*" the Sword shrieked in a sing-song voice as it slammed back into her, pushing her sideways. The sensation of having her spirit shoved was unlike anything she'd felt before, but it only disoriented her for a second.

"I don't care," Amy said, her voice loud and strong. "I don't care about you. I care about Connor. And I'm taking him back!"

"You do not know how this works, do you? Connor and I are one. We can never be separated, and if we are, he will die. But I will not."

She didn't flinch. "He may die, but at least he'll be free of you." She shot light at the shadowy figure. "I love him. I love Connor, and I'm going to set him free." Her golden energy began to glow a light pink at the ends. "I love him, and I am taking him *back*." The power exploded out of her again, and she heard the monster scream.

"What is this?" The inky shadow was speeding away from her, but she sent a thread of light from her hand to wrap around it and started to pull it back. *"What is this power?"* Her powers moved as an extension of her mind, completely one with her. *"IT BURNS."* The shadow struggled.

She pulled it to her, putting one hand over the other to drag it back like it was tied with rope.

As she pulled, the cord began to darken and turn gray. She stopped when it stung her hands but didn't let go. The darkness jumped from the rope and began to spread from her hands up her arms, burning her as it traveled. She gasped as pain shot throughout her. Her mind spun.

...Screeching metal then silence as her parents died.

...Adam stalked toward her, eyes glowing red.

...A doctor was telling her that her brother had been hurt.

Every painful memory she had slammed into her at once. She let go, put her hands over her face, and screamed.

"Yes, give in to the darkness," the Sword cooed as it began to wrap around her. *"Give in to the pain. Revel in it."* The glowing light faded, swallowed up by the darkness.

She stopped fighting. What was the point? Arty might be dead. Connor was gone. She couldn't fight this pain anymore. Her eyes closed.

"Amy..." Her eyes snapped open. She heard Connor's voice, weak, in the distance. "Amy..."

"Con...nor," she whispered.

"Amy!" She opened her eyes. Connor stood in front of her, hazy and indistinct. His body flickered.

"Connor?" The darkness pulsed around her, but its smothering embrace loosened.

"Amy," he said as he smiled at her. "I'm glad I get to see you one last time. I missed you."

"I love you!" she shouted. "I love you so much. I'm going to save you!" She reached out toward him, and pink and gold light shot from her body, piercing the darkness around her. Lunging toward him, she threw her arms around his form, barely able to feel him. *Is it because this is in our minds or is it...?*

"I love you too, Ames," he said. "I'm sorry I couldn't stop the Sword. I'm so sorry." The ghost of his arms wrapped delicately around her, and the faintest pressure on her head told her he'd rested his chin there. He pushed her back enough to look down at her. "But it's time for me to go."

"Connor, no!" She held on tighter but felt his presence fade. Looking up, she saw the shadows pulling him back as his silhouette blurred. "NO! GIVE HIM BACK!" Power blasted from her body. She sprang toward Connor, who appeared unconscious, and wrapped her arms around his waist. "You cannot have him!" she thundered. "You cannot have him or anyone else! I won't let you hurt anyone ever again!"

She encased Connor's sleeping form in a golden orb of light before turning on the shadow in front of her. Her voice rang out with the power and might of the Shield. It was amplified further by her love and the sheer force of her will.

"You are done, Sword. For millennia, you have plagued life. You have twisted and hurt countless people and ruined so many lives. You. Are. Finished." Bringing her arms behind her, she slammed them into each other in front of her in a thunderous clap. Her power shot from her and completely engulfed the shadow, caging it.

Its screams filled her ears before everything went black.

***

S HE OPENED HER EYES AND SAW CONNOR LYING ON the ground in front of her. His body was writhing as power surged around him. She ran to him and dropped to his side. The shadowy spirit was still in the cage of light on the spiritual plane, she could feel it, almost see it. *Get it out. I need to get it out of him.* Amy caught Connor's face in her hands and lowered her lips to his. She held him there as she inhaled and drew in the Sword's energy from deep within him and into herself.

The Sword and Shield's screams mingled inside of her as they were thrust together.

When she felt the last bit of darkness leave Connor's body, her own body felt like an overinflated balloon about to pop. Her head fell back, and her mouth opened in a silent scream. An inky, glowing mass of energy spewed forth, screeching. Spots danced in her vision as it choked her. She fell forward and caught herself on Connor's torso as the darkness left her.

Breathing hard, she threw a golden orb around herself and Connor, then looked up. The mass of shadows writhed and screamed above her, trying to flee.

"Oh no you don't!" she snapped, launching herself at it. She encased the entire shadow in a golden ball of light and crushed it inward.

"You're too weak to live outside a host or the spirit plane," she said through gritted teeth, fighting with everything she had to crush it further. "I won't let you escape! I won't let you hurt anyone else! You. Are. FINISHED."

She squeezed the orb as hard as she could with all of her power surrounding her. With a final squeak, the darkness vanished, and Amy dropped to the ground, lying on her back and looking up at the night sky. There were so many stars out. The cold of the ground seeped into her back.

Her eyes fluttered closed as exhaustion overtook her.

42

Amy

AMY WAS ALMOST WEIGHTLESS, BUT HER EYE-lids were heavy. It was a strange contrast, feeling both light and heavy, but it wasn't terrible. Soon a golden light filtered through her closed lids.

"Amy," came a soft voice. "Amy, wake up." With those simple words, her eyelids flew open as if released. A woman with olive skin and long black hair floated in front of her. She wore a white garment that looked ancient and timeless. However, unlike the last time Amy had seen her, she wore a gentle smile.

"Shield?" Amy whispered, confused. The woman chuckled. Amy's eyes widened.

"It is indeed me."

"But... what are you doing outside of me? I haven't seen you since the first day."

"We are on the spirit plane. This is the form of my first host. I find it the most comfortable one to assume. At least, until I met you. We had a natural, strong connection. I will miss it."

Amy stared with her mouth open for several long seconds. "Am I dead?"

The spirit smiled warmly at her. "No, you are not. You survived."

"But, what about the Sword?"

The spirit actually grinned, causing her eyes to light up. "You did it, Amy. You defeated the Sword."

"I did? But Connor—" The spirit held up a hand.

"Please, let me speak. I don't have much time." Amy closed her mouth. "You are the final incarnation of the Shield. After countless millennia and battles, the Sword was severely weakened. When you and its host combined forces against it and cast it out, it died. Your feelings for each other finally defeated the Sword. You were right to befriend the Sword boy all along. You are the first hosts to get to know each other, the first to love each other. Your connection to each other helped give you the strength to succeed." The spirit smiled again. "I have been so weary and have longed to return to my mother, the universe, and you have freed me. Thank you, Amy Sanders." The spirit bowed low, her hair almost touching the ground they stood on.

It was the first time Amy noticed they were standing on grass in a field that went as far as the eye could see. The sky around them was cloudless and peach colored, which cast a strange light on everything around it. She looked back at the spirit.

"But what about Connor? Is he alive too?"

The spirit frowned. "Yes and no." Amy opened her mouth to demand answers, but the spirit cut her off. "My mother is giving you three gifts in thanks for what you have done for us, for all life. Two of these gifts are true gifts, but I'm afraid the third will be a terrible burden. For the first gift, my mother has seen fit to revive the Sword bo—I mean Connor. He will survive." Amy let out an explosive breath of air, dropping to her knees in relief.

"Thank you," she choked out, her eyes shone as she looked up at the spirit.

The Shield nodded and continued. "The second gift is that my mother has done what she can to help your brother. He would have been paralyzed almost completely from the Sword's attack, but she has given him the power to heal. He will never be whole, but he may walk again one day." Hot tears streamed down Amy's cheeks. In the chaos of the night, she had almost forgotten about Arty being in the hospital.

"The third gift is a terrible burden, but I know you are strong enough to bear it. You, Amy Sanders, are the greatest Shield to ever live and Connor, the greatest Sword. The power that was once mine will live on inside both of you. The darkness may send another entity, and we need a first line of defense—that will be you two. You will be the Shields of Creation." Amy stared at her, and the Shield sighed. "I said the third gift would be a terrible burden, but it is the price of the first two."

Amy couldn't help but smile. "It's not a gift if you have to pay for it." The spirit tossed back her long mane of midnight hair and laughed, a merry sound. "But I accept."

"This is where I bid you farewell."

"What's going to happen to you?"

"I will go home to my mother and finally rest. Goodbye, Amy Sanders, and good luck." The spirit placed a hand on each side of her face and kissed her forehead. The spot she kissed became warm and the warmth spread through her body. The spirit began to fade.

"Goodbye, Shield," she whispered as the beautiful woman dissolved completely. As she vanished, the world around her began to swirl, and Amy felt herself being pulled downward. She screamed as the ground dropped away and she fell into darkness.

A MY GASPED FOR AIR, LUNGING UPWARDS, AND looked around wildly. She was sitting on the cold, hard ground in the physical world. The sky was pitch black, and the only thing illuminating the area was the faint light of the moon. She looked around until her eyes landed on Connor's still form a few feet from her. She tore grass from the ground in her hurry to get over to him.

She shook him. "Connor, wake up!" He didn't move, he didn't even look like he was breathing. Amy put her ear to his chest, but only heard silence. "Connor!" she yelled, shaking him harder.

The spirit's words replayed in the back of her mind. The power was for both of them. She looked down at her hands, which glowed gold.

"Of course," she whispered to herself. "He wasn't there. I need to give him the power." She laid him down and then bent over him. "Okay, Sleeping Beauty, let's see if this works."

She leaned down and kissed him, breathing into him, the opposite of when she had taken the Sword. Instinctively, she pulled power around herself and ordered half to flow from her mouth to his.

Connor glowed gold, and Amy sat back to watch him. He started to breathe, then sat bolt upright, gasping. He coughed and Amy pounded on his back, her smile wide.

"You're alive!" she exclaimed happily, throwing her arms around him when he finally stopped coughing. "I'm so happy." She squeezed him, reveling in how warm his body felt against hers, how alive he felt.

"I am?" he asked, confused. "I was sure I had died. I was sure I had killed you!" He turned to face her and pulled her in front of him in a graceless heap. "How are we alive?" Amy was surprised to see tears in his eyes and a look of pain on his face.

"The shortened version is that I killed the Sword, and as thanks, you're alive and we both have the power the Shield left behind in case the darkness sends a new emissary." Amy pushed him away and stood. "I'll explain more on the way, but right now, I need to go home and get ready to check on Arty. I need to go wait at the hospital."

Connor stared at her. "What happened to Arty?"

Amy grimaced. "The Sword attacked him to get at me." Connor's face paled, and he swayed. She steadied him with a hand on his arm. "It wasn't your fault. They did something to you to give the Sword control. You didn't do anything."

"I should have fought harder," he groaned, lowering his head and fisting both hands in his hair. "I swear, I will spend the rest of my life trying to make this up to you. I am so sor—" Amy threw her arms around him and kissed him deeply. He froze before relaxing and wrapping her up in his arms.

"It's alright Connor, you have nothing to be sorry for. We were pawns in a game, but we *won*. The Shield said if you hadn't fought so hard against the Sword, we'd both be dead. We saved each other, Connor. We did it." She shook him slightly, her face breaking out in a broad grin. "We won!"

He smiled. "I can't wait to see the look on my father's face when he finds out. Serves him right." Amy giggled. She held her hand out to him, and he took it, interlacing their fingers, his face softening as he looked at her. "I wanted to say this in the real world too. I love you, Amy Sanders."

Smiling, she stood up on her tiptoes to kiss him. "I love you too, Connor Callaghan," she said when they broke apart.

Holding hands, they walked out of the park just as the sun started to peak over the horizon. It had been the longest night of their lives, but they were alive. The morning light spilled over everything around them. They paused at the exit of the park to watch the sun shine down on a new day. There would be more battles ahead of them, but for tonight, this one was over.

They had won.

43
Connor

CONNOR STRODE DOWN THE FAMILIAR HOSPI-
tal corridor. The scents of disinfectant and poorly
made hospital food overwhelmed his senses. *This
place is the worst.* The fluorescent lights never failed to give
him a headache, but he kept his charming smile on for the
hospital staff despite it. He called out a hello and waved at a
nurse coming out of a private room. She turned and smiled
back at him.

"Hey, Connor, here to see your dad?" she asked, shut-
ting the door behind her carefully.

"Yes, ma'am. Has there been any change in him or the
others?" Connor worked his face into one of concern.

Sighing, she motioned for him to stand with her against
the wall, out of the way of a gurney being pushed by. "Sadly,
I'm afraid not. Your father and his friends are still unconscious. Our doctors here are keeping in contact with the

other doctors but…" She put a comforting hand on his arm. Long used to her, he didn't mind her touching him. "It doesn't look good." Connor forced his mouth to turn down at the corners. "They're deteriorating, and we don't know why." The only emotion he felt was grim satisfaction.

Connor patted her hand lightly. "It's okay, Nurse Jenny. It's been two months. My hopes aren't high."

She squeezed his arm and released it. "You've had a hard induction into adulthood—losing your mother when she kil–and now your father is… like this. How are you holding up?" Her face glowed with concern, reminding him of Amy.

He ran a hand through his hair, stomach squirming. "I luckily have a good support system, and my girlfriend convinced me to start therapy last week." He couldn't help the real smile that broke through when she crossed his mind. "I'm doing as well as can be expected."

"Good. If you ever need to talk, I'm always available. Go ahead and see your father. I've done all my checks, so you can have some alone time."

"Thank you, I won't be too long."

She patted his arm once more and walked away. Keeping his face neutral, Connor stepped into the dim, private room. He'd been shocked to learn that Whittaker Hills General had private rooms available. His father could rot in a ditch for all he cared, but appearances were appearances.

The machines hooked up to his father beeped continuously as he lay there. His sharp cheekbones stood out more so in his now gaunt face. Those hands which had always filled Connor with fear were withered and weak looking. Connor couldn't help the sneer that crossed his face as he continued his perusal, disgust filling him.

"Hello, Father," he said at last. "Just stopping by to keep up the façade, you know how it is." He flopped into a chair near the end of the bed, immediately disliking the hard seat. "I do wish you and the others would hurry it along so you can join Mother in Hell. I tire of playing the loving son when we both know there was never any love between us." Leaning forward, he rested his elbows on his thighs. "*We* won. You lost, Father. You and the Sheath—you all lost." Sitting up, he summoned a gold orb of light into his hand. It was wonky, but he smiled at it anyway.

"I belong in the light, with Amy. I almost wish I could see your face when you learn that your precious host now serves the universe as a Shield instead of the Sword you were so proud of." He clenched his hand, extinguishing the orb. "But at the rate you're going, you'll never get that chance." Checking his watch, he stood and stretched. "That should be enough time. Enjoy your slow demise, Father. I won't mourn you when you pass."

As he turned to leave, he froze. His eyes widened and fixed onto where Preston's hand lay, still and withered. Ice coursed through his veins, and his heart pounded as he stared at the hand for several long minutes. Finally, he left, stomach in knots and breathing slightly erratic. Preston's hand had stayed still as he watched it, but Connor could have sworn he saw a finger move.

Amy's Sketchbook

Arty and Amy

Satomi and Adam

Connor

Amy and Connor

WANT TO GET IN TOUCH?

Thank you so, so much for making it to the end of my book! If you're willing, I would greatly appreciate a review on Goodreads, Amazon, or anywhere else you want to review my book.

I'm super active across multiple social media platforms and try to reply to every comment I get on them. You can find links to all my accounts, see what I'm working on, subscribe to my newsletter (I send it out like, once a quarter and on special occasions), contact me directly, and more at:

WWW.ALEXASHAYS.COM

I look forward to getting to know you if you connect with me on social media. I try to follow back other bookish accounts as much as possible, because the online book community is generally wonderful. Until next time!

ACKNOWLEDGEMENTS

A book is nearly impossible to bring into the world by oneself. These are some people who helped make my dream of publishing a book come true.

I would like to thank fellow indie author, Eloise Bahr, for all the help she gave me in starting this adventure and during it. We participated in NaNoWriMo 2017 together (I no longer support that organization) and we've bounced a lot of ideas off each other. Some of the concepts used came from her mind, including the original idea for the cover art. Thank you, Eloise, for being an amazing best friend.

Next, this book would never have become what it is today without the incredible help and dedication of Hazel Halloway. She read the first ever draft (which was hot garbage) and helped me a lot with honing my vision. She supported me, cheered me on, became very invested in my world, and helped me when I doubted myself. Thank you for being my friend in all things and sorry about (spoiler alert) Arty.

A massive shout out to my editor Brittany Ortega of E&A Editing Services. She helped me learn a lot about the craft of writing, pushed me to be better, and put up with my whining. She was instrumental in transforming me from a wannabe into a full-fledged, published author.

A huge thanks to Karri Klawiter (www.artbykarri.com) for making my amazing book cover and all of its related promo materials—it's even better than I dreamed! She was amazing to work with and I highly recommend her to anyone looking to have a book cover made.

An additional thank you is owed to another of my best friends, Jennifer (who I call Jeniveve and yes, I know that's spelled wrong and no, I don't care.), who helped make sure the few medical scenes in my book were mostly realistic. Thank you for always being there for me and helping talk me down when I get all wound up from anxiety.

I should probably thank my husband too. Thanks for always supporting my crazy dreams, Lovebug, even when they take up a lot of time and money. I love you... most of the time.

ABOUT THE AUTHOR

Technical writer by day and creative writer by night, Alexa Shay is an author and award-winning public speaker from Western Washington, USA. She's a massive nerd/geek/dork and has been working on her debut novel (this novel) off and on in one way or another since she was a child. She looks forward to not reading it again for a while now that it's published (for the uninformed, one must read their book many, *many* times before it's ready for publication. Even then, you can miss things.).

In her free time, she enjoys reading fantasy and romance books, taking care of her high-maintenance cats, and doing a ton of different crafting hobbies. Choosing just one hobby is impossible when there are so many out there!